I0780337

E. S. MAGILL, EDITOR

FEATURING

MIKE D. MCCARTY

VANESSA FOGG

ERIC J. GUIGNARD

KC GRIFANT

JOHN PALISANO

KATHRYN BLANCHE

VINCENT V. CAVA

JON COHN

DAVID AGRANOFF

An Anthology of
Horror Science-Fiction Stories

E.S. MAGILL, EDITOR

Gramarye Press
2025

TITLE: *SPACE HORRORS: An Anthology of Horror Science Fiction Stories*
EDITOR: E.S. Magill
PAPERBACK ISBN: 978-1-961502-12-3
GENRE: Fiction | Anthology | Short Stories   Horror | Science Fiction | Space Horror

For information about rights and permissions, contact:
Scribes & Scribblers Publishing
www.scribesandscribblerspub.com

Scribes & Scribblers Publishing
12621 N Tatum Blvd #1782
Phoenix, AZ 85032

Book cover design | GR Book Covers

Graphics | depositphotos.com

CONTENTS

E.S. MAGILL

INTRODUCTION

HORROR REACHES FOR THE STARS

SPACE AND HORROR seem a natural pairing: the infinite void, the unknown, the cold silence, the terror of what might be lurking in the dark between the stars. However, as I began writing this introduction on space horror, I noticed a curious absence: space horror, which is horror set in space, has been rare among horror authors, especially in novel form.

We should start by defining space horror, horror science fiction, and science fiction horror. The distinction between horror science fiction and science fiction horror may seem like wordplay, but conceptually the two subgenres differ. Think of *Alien* directed by Ridley Scott in which he describes the film as "*The Texas Chainsaw Massacre* of science fiction," making *Alien* a horror science fiction narrative and, more specifically, a space horror narrative as its setting is outer space. Science fiction horror, on the other hand, is a story where the genre tropes and ideas are foremost science fiction, with horror elements woven in. The second movie in the franchise *Aliens* is a science-fiction action epic with monsters, not a horror film set in space. One note, space horror does not have to take place in outer space but can also occur on alien planets, moons, or some other outpost.

Despite my claim that space horror isn't common among horror authors, classic works of horror with an outer space twist abound, though they typically feature Earth as the setting. The H.P. Lovecraft canon of Cosmic Horror is rooted in the idea of unfathomable beings from the stars; yet while his stories originate out there, they occur here on our terrestrial sphere. Also, Lovecraft's oeuvre is comprised of short stories and novellas, not novels. Jack Finney's novel *Invasion of the Body Snatchers* is about an extraterrestrial threat, but the nightmare unfolds in small-town America. John Wyndham's *The Midwich Cuckoos* and Michael Crichton's *Sphere* and *The Andromeda Strain* center on terrors that have come to us, not the other way around. Aside from Lovecraft, these authors aren't horror writers. If you were to consider a classic horror writer before 1980, could you recall a horror novel set in space by any of them? The list comes up short. Even George R.R. Martin, who began his career with a more horror-leaning bent, only dipped his pen into space horror with the novel *Nightflyers* (based on a short story) in 1981. Meanwhile, science fiction writers such as Greg Bear, Alan Dean Foster, and Philip K. Dick have crafted stories with strong horror elements, but their reputations reside in the realm of science fiction.

Interestingly, films have been far more daring in exploring space horror. The *Alien* series, *Event Horizon*, *Pitch Black*, and a host of 1950s and 60s B-movies (*The Thing From Another World*, *Forbidden Planet, Planet of the Vampires*) have all shown us that space is an endless source of dread. Surprisingly, several horror franchises have taken to space: *Leprechaun 4 In Space; Hellraiser: Bloodline; Jason X*; and, yes, *Critters 4*.

Many of these space horror films have been turned into novelizations and tie-ins and often so at the hands of science fiction writers. Alan Dean Foster, not known for horror, wrote the novelizations for *Alien* and *Aliens*, but traditional horror authors have been invited to continue the canonical *Alien* franchise: Tim Lebbon, Weston Ochse, Yvonne Navarro, Mary Sangiovanni, among others. While more horror science fiction rather than space horror, the *Predator* franchise also turned to horror authors for adaptations and original stories, writers such as James A. Moore and Christopher Golden. As for the aforementioned space horror movies, Pat Cadigan, who's made her mark in horror and fantasy, novelized *Jason X*, and Peter Atkins, who wrote the screenplays for three of the *Hellraiser* movies, released the original screenplay for the fourth film, *Bloodline*, in book form. Horror authors have written space horror, but often within the boundaries of established film franchises.

Which brings us to the short story form and this book you hold in your hands. So while I've been pointing out the lack of space horror novels, horror writers have penned space horror in short form. One of my writing partners (M.D.) pointed to Stephen King's "Beachworld" from his collection *Skeleton Crew* (1985), and when I picked up the book to refresh my memory, I rediscovered "The Jaunt." There's Lovecraft, of course. Richard Matheson published *The Shores of Space,* 1957. And here are two modern anthologies featuring space horror—from 2023, The *Darkness Beyond the Stars: An Anthology of Space Horror* edited by P.L. McMillan and, from 2021, *Midnight From Beyond the Stars* edited by Kenneth W. Cain. Both contain space horror stories by notable horror writers.

This anthology, *Space Horrors*, is a product of convention shop talk, whereby I declared, "There isn't enough space horror." Everyone within earshot agreed. I can now, however, understand why so many horror writers are hesitant to venture into the subgenre; it's not easy writing in a genre that demands the science be accurate (science fiction) and in another genre requiring that special

4

sauce which makes horror one of the most difficult forms to nail. And, once again, *Space Horrors* takes on space horror in the familiar short story mode.

So what about space horror novels? Within the past two decades, a new wave of horror writers has boldly ventured where so few have gone. Caitlin Starling's Stoker-nominated *The Luminous Dead*, S.A. Barnes's *Dead Silence*, and Dave Wellington's *The Last Astronaut* are all recent examples of authentic horror set in space. And John Palisano, a contributor to this anthology, has now joined the space horror canon with his novel *Requiem*. These works don't bring the horror to Earth but instead launch us into the cosmic unknown. Horror writers are making headway into the realm of space horror novels, which will make this introduction irrelevant, or at least an artifact, in less than a decade. About time!

Why has space horror been a relatively new genre for horror authors? Even from the beginning, science fiction was no stranger to horror—*Frankenstein, Dr. Jekyll & Mr. Hyde, The Island of Dr. Moreau*—as the ramifications of science can be, well, horrific. Today's horror genre, however, descends from the Gothic, whose tropes consist of decaying mansions, misty moors, ancient tomes, ghostly apparitions. Nowhere in the tradition lies science, which is a convention adopted as the genre expanded into its present form. Perhaps it is only now, as our civilization moves into the realities and possibilities of space travel that horror writers feel it's time to move beyond our familiar world. The unknown is the purest source of fear, and there is no greater unknown than outer space.

While some stories in this anthology are frightening, some are also humorous. They all, however, examine horrors familiar to the human experience: the mysteries of the universe, the brutality of the unknown species, depression, alien sex and human kink, lifeform manipulation, unregulated science, rogue AI, crime and punishment, sentient lifeforms beyond our comprehension, and the ultimate of all horrors, the evil humans do to other humans. You will find stories in these pages that don't just import terrors to Earth. Instead, they draw the reader into the abyss of out there to face nightmares and, eventually, ourselves.

— E.S. Magill

SPACE HORRORS

There's no horror here we don't create ourselves.

—from *Galaxy of Terror*

SPACE HORRORS

VANESSA FOGG

SPACE HORRORS

THE SPACE ROADS

VANESSA FOGG

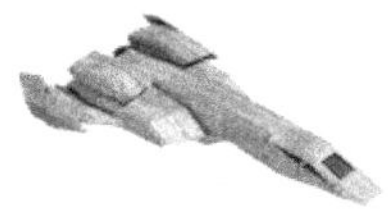

THE STATION GREETER:
THERE'S A LOOK THAT LONG-HAUL pilots all get. A worn, haunted look, shadows ringing the eyes. It comes from too much time in the void, in the blackness between stars. Feet that touch no earth, no solid rock. Lungs that go too long without the sweet breath of a real planetary atmosphere. It gets to you, after a while. And all the best simulations in the galaxy—that best-selling immersion of the paradise-gardens of Elysium, those lapping blue waves on the sugar-sand beaches of Lantian, the perfect virtual recreation of your favorite spot on your own home-world—none of that is enough.

Yeah, I see it in your eyes. Sit down, kid. Take a load off. The beer here is good, and Auntie Ting—back there in the kitchen—serves the best noodle soups on this route, from the Adamite Jump Gate to Xanadu. Real wheat noodles. Heirloom chilis and herbs grown right here on the station. And the flavor of her beef stock? As close to real beef as you can get out here, as far out in the deeps as we are.

We're all friendly—mostly long-haulers like you. Some have been stuck on this deep-space station for a while, what with the trouble at the Xanadu Gate messing up all the shipping routes. It's nice to see a new face. Hear some new stories. Get the latest news from the deeps. It's been a long, long time since I was out there myself. It's my job now to welcome all travelers, from long-haul pilots like you to long-haul business commuters and starry-eyed tourists on their first space jump. I'm here to help you feel at home. To help you shake off, for a bit, the cold of deep space.

Hey, there's the old crew over at the corner table. Jak, the old blowhard, been hauling cargo ships longer than anyone. Su, legend and queen of the deeps. And Cal, a youngster like you, just started yesterday! (I'm kidding). Cal, my man, how you doing? What are we having, everyone?

Ah. It's Cal's ghost stories on the menu tonight. Monsters and things that go boo in the dark. He'll swear that each and every one is true.

CAL (not a youngster but a lean man of around 40-years standard, brown hair turning to gray, but with an earnest manner that still vibrates with the wide-eyed intensity of youth):

Ah, shut it, old man. Don't mind him, kid—tell the Greeter to kick it if he gets on your nerves. He's retired from the space-routes, hasn't hauled cargo in years. Cushy job here now on the station, telling old stories and buying us drinks.

And no, I don't believe every story I tell. This is just talk over beers, you know? Some fun to pass the time. But I wouldn't say they're all not true, either.

You know what stories you should always suspect? The ones they tell you that you must believe. The ones you're not allowed to question. The official party line.

Take this: there's been an increase in missing ships. Everyone knows it. Ships disappearing right into the void. Somewhere between Gates the signal is lost, and nothing—no beacon call, no salvage, no trace—is ever found. Pirates, the authorities say. And I'm not saying that doesn't happen. There've always been pirates, and hard times and war make it worse.

But there's more to it than that. A class A6 Behemoth on a well-marked route disappearing whole without warning? Without time for a distress call—nothing at all? Gone just like that?

Big ships and small, the cargo haulers, passenger cruisers—even a military craft or two. Bet you didn't know about that last, huh? Yeah, I've got my sources. They keep it hushed up, but some of us have our ears to the sky.

It's increasing. They will say there's no statistical increase, nothing over any other standard cycle. They're lying. They can publish all the official reports they want. I know the truth.

There's something out there. Something not human. Something that's swallowing ships.

And no, I'm not talking about "monsters." Not like the Greeter here is saying. Not mythical space krakens, not the zombie reavers of childhood tales. Not escaped and malfunctioning mech-monsters, or even remnants of alien civilizations come back to life.

No, this is something . . .else.

Some rip in space-time itself. A flux in the darkness. A dip in the road that you don't see until too late. Until you fall in, and it grips you, and you can't get out.

The space-roads are old, far older than we know. These relics of a dead empire, crisscrossing space-time. Safe paths through the chaos and night. We think we've mapped them all, that we control the routes and Gates. That we know how it works.

But there's a void built in that we don't understand. An emptiness woven into the very fabric of space-time. Sometimes it frays. Sometimes

14

the road crumbles. I think there are more and more places where the roads are crumbling, where it's all coming apart. They don't want you to know. They want us to pretend that it's okay. That if we just stick to our routes and do what we're told, the ships and cargo will get there on time. And that's still mostly true.

Until it's not.

SU (a woman about Cal's age, short-cropped hair and an impish light in her eyes. A low voice and confiding air as she leans forward with her tale):

Cal's right, you know? Not about everything, of course. Not about a lot, actually (teasing glance across the table). But he's right on some of this. Ships are going missing. I don't know if it's more than usual, or not. But they've always gone missing, and it's something more than pirates. Something more than human accident or action.

The spookiest part is when the ships are found again.

You've all heard the stories of ghost ships. The signal of a ship ahead on the road. It's distant, a full standard planetary system away. But the signal's clear as a sun, unmistakable—right there. You watch it getting ever closer on your screen. But just as you come up on it, it's gone. As abruptly and completely as falling through a Gate—though of course there's no Gate for light-years around. It's like the ship fell through—what did Cal call it? A dip in the road. A distortion of space-time. A rip in the fabric of things.

It was there, then it wasn't. And when you search, there's no report of any such ship on the route at the time. Or any report of any ship anywhere disappearing then.

A glitch in your instrument sensors? But it's not. Everything's working just fine.

A glitch in your brain? Stress and fatigue? You thought you saw something, but you didn't. Your ship has no recording of it at all. You're just tired. You need a break—to get to a station or planetside quick. You need the company of others, a good hot-cooked meal, the close light of a sun. Maybe the touch of a real breeze, a real sky overhead, green plants and grass under your feet.

That's what we tell ourselves, anyway, when it happens.

But there are also real ghost ships out there, with known names and histories. Ships that really did exist and really disappeared. *Red Hawk*, *Enchantment*, *Bright Pulsar*, and *Foregone Conclusion*. Ships that continue to signal from the deeps. Pilots report picking up their exact signatures, near the places where they were last seen. But the signals are coming from outside the space roads—they're in the darkness that runs like black rivers alongside.

Sometimes there's an actual distress call. Sometimes, pilots report, they hear actual voices on the audio channel. Human voices crackling with static, voices laughing, arguing, speaking conversationally. A child's voice crying on the *Enchantment*. A woman singing on *Bright Pulsar*. Voices low and distant, just under the threshold of understanding. Turn up the volume and it all breaks into static, to white noise.

There are reports of pilots who claim to have turned off-course, who pursued these signals into the dark. Adventurers looking for a story. Would-be heroes. And some perhaps just caught up in a mystery, in the lure of the deeps.

There's a guy in the Gliese star system who's still telling his story over rounds of drinks, telling it to whoever will listen. He says he followed the call of the *Enchantment* off-route until he saw the ship with his own eyes. All the lights were still on. All systems running. It looked just like its old holo-vids—the famous luxury passenger liner, the biggest of its age. Brimming with light and life, after three-hundred standard years.

But he never got any closer. He could see the *Enchantment* with his eyes; he could see its position on his screen. He heard music from the luxury liner. He heard voices, low and indistinct, on his comms. But it was as though he were trapped in glass, and on the other side of the glass was the ship, impossibly fixed in place. He couldn't move forward. His ship was somehow frozen. He could only turn back.

There are scattered reports of sightings of other missing ships. Of *Foregone Conclusion*, cold and dark, not a mark on the military vessel, no sign of damage. No sign of life. No clue as to what led the ship off-road, or of what happened to its people. Pilots say that, as with the *Enchantment* and others, the ship is fixed in place, as if pinned to its position by a great cosmic needle. And it's impossible to reach, as though sealed off in a bubble of space-time.

There are stories of pilots who left to explore these haunted ships and never came back. Their ships, too, might be out there in bubbles of their own, silent or alive, floating in the void off the marked roads.

JAK (a man of around sixty-years standard; thoughtful eyes in a long, lined face; a slow, quiet yet emphatic manner of speaking):
People lose their minds out in deep space.

I've been around long enough to see it. Been long-hauling cargo since I was seventeen. I've seen old veterans of the roads—my own mentors—go mad. Come close to it myself.

What do you think these stories are, of pilots chasing shadows off-route? Ghost sightings that no auto-ship-logs ever record. That no instrumentation records ever confirm. Things seen and heard only by a pilot flying single, overworked and alone too many days in the dark.

It gets to you, the road. Slowly. You don't even notice. Static on the comms channel, glitches in the machinery. That's normal. Then there are the knocks and creaks—that's fine, too. But you find yourself crawling through the ship, trying to track down the source of the knocking sound for the fiftieth time, and you can't. System checks find nothing. You start to think there's something wrong with the overall system, with the diagnostic programs themselves. The ship's lying to you. Through every speaker, its voice sounds mocking. When messages arrive from company headquarters, they all sound mocking, too. There are shadows—quick movements—in the corner of your eye. Something just vanished around the corner of a room. It was there—you barely missed it. You feel your heart racing. You hear the sound of breathing that's not your own. There's someone else, something else, in the ship with you. When you try to sleep, you can feel its eyes on your face.

From the beginning, pilots have reported such symptoms: paranoia, delusions, and outright hallucination. They can occur anywhere between Gates, anywhere on the deep roads. But have you ever noticed where they most often occur? Where the most reported human breakdowns happen?

Cal and Su are both right: there are "haunted" places in space. Spots where the roads crumble and ghost ships appear. Where people see and hear things that can't be confirmed.

I don't think it's all madness. I mean it is, but I think there's more.

There's something about the way these regions in space interact with our brains. Something about human consciousness itself. It's only our consciousness, after all, that can unlock the Gates. And it's only our bio-minds that can navigate the roads, keep the ship straight and true. No artificial intelligence, no ship-computer alone, has ever managed it, despite all the money spent trying.

And where the road gets worn away? Where space-time gets bent, where it dips and twists? Our brains interact with that, too.

It's what Su said about "bubbles of space-time." There are weird bubbles you can slide into. Pocket dimensions. A pilot's brain can slip into it without even knowing. And I think. . . it's not all in the head. That interaction between a human brain and a distortion of space-time? It creates its own reality.

I'll never forget this one story. It's about a guy I knew, steadiest person around. Last person you would think to succumb to the void. Met him when we were both doing the New Atlantis route. There was a minor insurrection at the Atlantis gate—like the troubles around Xanadu now—and we were stuck for nearly a year at Vermillion Station 5. Rations ran low, fights broke out. Things got downright hairy. I won't go into details. But this guy—my friend—he kept it together. He kept us all together. I never saw him lose his cool. A natural leader, and we needed one then. Didn't surprise me when I learned later that he'd been a combat pilot in the First Cygnus Wars. An honest-to-gods war hero, medals and all. He never talked about it.

It was years later that the thing happened. We were working different routes then, hadn't seen each other in some time. He was on the run between Eden and the Penglai Gate. He got a signal on his screen: a fellow cargo ship just off-road. Calling for help.

A ship that looked like his. Same company and make.

The identity signature seemed familiar. It was a moment before he realized—it was his ship's identity call.

He opened a comm channel and hailed it. No response.

He sent a message to headquarters and another to a friend. Then he followed the other ship off-road.

I don't know what he was thinking. I don't know why he did it; he should have just kept going. He knew the reputation of that stretch of road; he knew the stories. And he knew that time is money: he had a schedule to keep to, cargo to run. Was he trying to be a hero again?

He turned off the well-marked route, into the darkness.

He went on until he saw the ship with his own unaided eyes. He said that it was his ship, exactly. The name blazoned on its body, the registration code on the tail. The pattern of thermal paint, and even the pitting on one side—light damage from a debris accident which he'd yet to fix.

It was his own ship before him: silent, unresponsive, cold. No systems running, no sign of life.

He flew to it in his own warm ship, and from his ship's chair he sent two last messages. He said he was boarding his ship's silent twin. "I'm going in," he said. His voice was eerily calm.

A few minutes later: "I'm in," he said. No inflection at all in his tone.

And that's the last I ever heard from him.

THE STATION GREETER:

It's true. I remember when *The Herald* disappeared. No trace was ever found. I'm sorry, Jak.

Oh, you don't know the story, kid? Well, it was before you were born. Just another strange tale from the space roads. An unexplained disappearance, a warning tale from the deeps. A real person lost.

Jak and others talk of danger spots on the routes. But it's all dangerous, of course. We just try not to think of it. It's what you do to go on.

Some say the danger's been seeded from the start. We humans were never meant to be traveling deep space. The system of Gates and routes wasn't meant for us. Our neurological systems aren't truly equipped. We're supposed to be planetside, in the orbit of a star, breathing real air and feeling earth-gravity under our feet. Some go even further: they say we should have never left Mother Earth at all.

I don't go with that last, of course—I'm not a fanatic. But . . . spending too much time in the void is dangerous, wherever you are and whatever route you take. All that distance between stars. All that emptiness and space. The human mind can't process it—we're not supposed to. We're supposed to block it out. And we mostly do, successfully.

Until something happens—too much time in the dark, some hidden vulnerability triggered, and the void leaks in like an infection through a cut.

And then a person might fly their ship off into the darkness. They might take a whole ship of passengers with them. They might sabotage their own life support systems, depressurize the cabin, start a fire, or step out through an airlock unsuited. They might board a station and attack staff and guests, run amok through the corridors and try their best to disable the power arrays.

But that's not happening tonight, of course. Hey, we're all just telling stories, here on the station all cozy and warm. Drink up, kid, this last one's on me. You look tired. After this, I'll show you to your room.

***

Well, here you are. Standard station room—you'll be familiar with all the settings. And look, there's even a little plant—a fern?—in the corner under the growth light there. Bit of green for your room.

One last thing before I say goodnight.

You've been in the deeps too long, kid. I can see it in your eyes. I didn't want to say it in front of the others, but I think they saw it too. A worn, haunted look. The void peering out.

I know you've been told to stay here until the Xanadu Gate reopens, but I don't think you have time. You should get planetside now. Cielo-2 isn't far. Fuck what your company says. I'll vouch for you in a letter; I'm a Station-Greeter and this is my job.

Rest here tonight, but in the morning head to Cielo. Check into one of Var Port's cheap lodgings. Breathe in the soft air, walk around a bit. Go visit one of Var's famous parks. Take off your shoes and feel the grass under your feet.

Let the void leak out. Stay there, on the planet, until it does.

Hey, I'll see you off in the morning. And I'll order you one of Auntie Ting's soup bowls, for the road.

THE DIRECTIVE

MIKE D. McCARTY

SPACE HORRORS

THE DIRECTIVE

MIKE D. MCCARTY

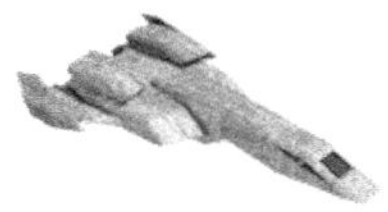

THE MIND, WHEN SUSPENDED in hypersleep, is like a never-ending dream that, when one comes out of it, slowly crumbles away like a sandcastle under the oncoming tide of wakefulness.

The frosted polycarbonate cover of the Paulson Systems 3000 hypersleep pod slowly lifted with a whir. The air lines disconnected, completing their service with the loud snap of compressed air. Inside the chamber, he struggled to sit up, meeting a slight tugging resistance from the heart and vital organ leads connected to him. He peeled them off his pasty, sweat-dampened skin and dropped them loose in the pod.

He paused for a moment and looked around. The ship was dark, and the room cast in an ominous red glow.

Emergency power? Battle stations?

There were no usual red flashing lights or warning klaxons that would accompany the ship being on a battle station's alert.

Wait, no, not battle stations, this was a supply ship.

That knowledge surprised him. Although his mind was emerging from beneath the fog of hypersleep, he still felt more disoriented than usual, as if he couldn't harness his own brain. From the Paulson input training, he remembered the questions:

What's your name?

I'm...

Three shapes danced around his mind. He grasped for them, but they seemed distant, beyond his reach.

I'm— Hell, I don't know my name.

Where are you?

I know I'm on a Paulson Systems supply ship, The Cerberus, to deliver a shipment to Torin Prime Station. It was a typical mining station load of carbon scrubbers, drill tips, mail, and dry goods. But something else too… What was it?

It washed in fast and hard with the tide of memories.

Yes. There it was. Triton 6 fuel rods. Paulson Systems' latest. Triton 6 was a revolutionary new, cleaner-burning, longer-lasting fuel rod that the company had come up with, real secretive stuff. There had been threats as other companies like Santo Corp tried to deconstruct it for the formula.

He tried the next question: What day is it?

That's a stupid question. Out here in space, there are no calendar days._Time is measured in work shifts and flight rate.

The next question was the real issue: What's happening?

Good question. What is happening? Pirates? That was possible for a supply ship run. Occasionally, they embedded Marines for protection, but this was a small crew. If others had taken over the ship, where were they?

He looked around, more puzzled. He knew there were a total of eight crew aboard, including himself. He held his breath and listened for a sound, any sound at all, but there was nothing, nothing beyond the droning white noise of the ship's impulse engines.

It was dead silent, like a galactic tomb.

Why am I even in hyper?

In a fleeting moment of panic, he patted his body down to see if he was wounded, but everything seemed fine. Again, he looked left, then right, letting his eyes adjust to the lighting.

He thumbed his eye sockets and massaged up to his temple, then brushed his fingers hard against his scalp, pushing back his medium-length brown hair. His brain was still in a fog of the Paulson suspension chemicals that had put him under, so little was coming back to him or making sense. He knew it was common to come out of hypersleep foggy and unaware of one's surroundings. A lot of people had forgetfulness. They called it hyper-dementia. A temporary amnesia that didn't usually last too long but was always a little unnerving to the sleeper who struggled to remember what was going on, who they were, or why they were here. The PS cell boosters, administered via the hyper-pod upon waking, helped, but it wasn't a definitive fix.

30

Mostly, they dealt with the nausea and muscular atrophy that came with a long hypersleep.

But the way his brain felt scrambled. This wasn't just hyper-dementia, which he'd experienced before. No, this seemed like something else, something beyond his control.

He sat for a second and thought. He remembered being part of the crew. They had left Sawyer Station with a full complement. Their mission was mostly the Triton 6 rods. He was sure he had been one of the two pilots. A ship like a PS-Buffalo-09 Supply Cruiser didn't need two pilots on board. They practically flew themselves with nav systems and auto-docking, but Paulson Systems Corporation regulations stated two pilots needed to be on every ship in case there was a ship-wide systems failure of the autopilot or if the first pilot was incapacitated. The company set everything up redundantly. Everybody had two jobs. The Chief Med-tech Officer was also in charge of communications, and the communications officer had more medical training than your average shipmate.

He stretched his arms up high to get the blood moving and then vigorously shook his head. Some of the fog was beginning to dissipate.

Why is it so quiet? Where is everyone? Are they all in stasis?

He looked around the room, awash in its ominous red glow. His eyes began to adjust a bit more to being awake.

How long has it been?

He wasn't completely atrophied, so it couldn't have been that long, but his mind felt like it had been longer than normal.

Aside from the emergency power glow, nothing else appeared out of place. He slowly slipped his legs over the hypersleep module's edge and stepped towards the floor. His bare foot skimmed something irregular and ice-cold. He recoiled in horror and looked down to see a withered human form, its dark, leathery arm at an odd angle, thin fingers reaching forward, grasping at nothing, frozen in terror.

Hypoxia?

He clocked the O2 sensor on the wall. No. Green. So the air was clean.

He stared down at the body on the floor. Its face was destroyed beyond recognition; someone or something had smashed it repeatedly into the pod side. It was then he noticed the rusty brown smears on the pod cover that had kept him safe in stasis.

He cautiously stepped over the corpse and planted himself firmly onto the cold floor. A locker
32

stood half open, and he headed towards it. He shook his arms to get the blood moving. It was cold, not freezing cold, but not comfortable either.

Inside the locker was a standard ship's uniform. It wouldn't keep him warm, but it would help until he investigated the temperature control systems. The basic uniform was a medium-size jumper in light gray with a blue stripe down the side. The stripe signified…

What was it? Security detail?

In the low light he had to squint to read the stitched-on name. It was simple, BOB in all caps. He stuffed in one leg and balanced as he put the other in. The jumper slid on cleanly, and he found he could zip it up the chest with no issue.

"I guess I'll be Bob."

The sound of his own voice almost spooked him; it rang hollow in the quiet. He moved slowly around the room, getting his bearings. His bare foot caught something, and it slid across the floor as he kicked it. He reached down and picked it up. The touch pad slowly blinked to life.

A Personnel Data Transmitter.

The battery lit up amber, still registering a little power. These things could go dormant for years. Most crew members kept theirs on them. But they were versatile enough that it would log itself to the user who was holding it at the time, so a person didn't necessarily have to have their own. It would capture the user's body chemistry and immediately lock in on that person until they turned it over to someone else. It was so sensitive that the moment it transferred hands, it would lock onto the new holder. The Paulson System's screen came to life with the company ID number PS-B-09-808, but no name. The health monitor looked clean; nothing seemed strange. He breathed a sigh of relief.

Was this one mine?

He looked at the withered body near the pod. "Maybe it's yours?" He checked the messages and camera settings and found a video. He hit play.

It was obviously shot in a hurry while the person was running. The video had a panic-stricken view, bouncing up and down. A familiar voice panted nearly out of breath, "They're after me, I gotta, I gotta find a spot, find a place, I need a weapon." The camera whipped back and forth. "They're killing us all." The voice was panicked.

The camera view ducked under what appeared to be a maintenance rack and then started sliding along the floor. It came to a complete stop with an angled but clear look across the floor to the door. The camera owner was quiet but still panting, trying to control their breath.

The door on the far end slid open with a whoosh, but the camera saw only the crewmember's legs and feet. This person stepped into the room with a slow and steady determination. And said in another familiar voice, "I know you're in here. You can't hide from me. Your PDT is pinging you in this room."

The form moved steadily towards the shelving unit, and without a pause, reached down and hauled out whoever was running the camera. The camera at this point was cast off to the side, showing nothing but the base of the lockers, although it continued recording the sounds of the struggle. "I'm sorry it must be this way. You must be eliminated."

The voice was drowned out by the screams as the person was dragged out of the room.

The next sound was a heavy, wet thump — and another and a third. Each time, the agony of the victim got weaker as the banging echoed down the empty walls. The wet smashes continued to reverberate until the groans stopped. Then, a pause, as if the camera was waiting or thinking or something, followed by footsteps walking away, and nothing. About a minute of excruciating silence passed before the camera powered down to sleep mode.

He slowly lowered the PDT, a wave of nausea washed over him. Filling his dry mouth with spit. He had always been against violence, even just hearing the atrocity sent a chill down his spine. He tapped the screen again, bringing up the ship's crew locator. A green blueprint of the ship appeared with all the systems and rooms labeled. Normally, the locator would be full of blips for crew members with their tagged PDTs. A crewmember could tap a blip to bring up whoever it was, but the screen was empty, no one was pinging. It didn't necessarily mean that there wasn't anyone alive on the ship; it could be that there was somebody alive on the ship who just didn't have a PDT with them. Some crew members didn't like the intrusiveness of having something on them all the time that could pinpoint their location, especially if people were going off to another part of the ship they didn't want anyone to know about. These were typically intimate moments, someone going off to fraternize with another crew member.

He turned around and saw the maintenance shelf where the crewmember had been hiding under. He exited through the door he had seen in the video and found small splashes of rusty brown spattering the floor, like someone had shaken a paintbrush. This led the way to another body.

This one's arm was torn off, and the back bent at a horribly broken angle. This corpse, too, was withered and desiccated like the other. The climate on the ship had kept it somewhat preserved so that the decomposition of the bodies had been very little. But it was too hard to tell how long it had been there. He looked up from the body.

Something appeared to be written on the wall, but in the emergency power lighting, it was hard to make out. He turned the PDT's flashlight towards the words, and the hand-scrawled letters popped out immediately.

THE DIRECTIVE ISSS

The finger-painted scratchings of the unknown artist appeared to have been written in the blood of the crewmember sprawled awkwardly on the floor. Whoever wrote it carried on the s of what appeared to say *The Directive Is.*

What Directive?

He continued out of the room and down the deck to the main maintenance area. A lot of the ship's systems could be monitored from there. There were redundant setups for controlling nearly everything ship-wide. He cautiously made his way down the hallways, ducking under bulkheads as he passed into separate, dimly lit corridors. Most of the doors were hauntingly open like yawning mouths of the unknown in a nightmare. The lighting was consistent throughout the ship, a soft red glow leading the way towards the emergency exits.

Bob always thought it amusing to have the exits lit while underway. It wasn't like a person could really get off the ship unless they were docked somewhere.

There must be someone else here...unless they escaped.

The ship's layout appeared in his mind: On the third floor near the galley there were four 2-man escape pods.

He made his way to the ship's transit elevator, normally used for transferring heavy equipment from floor to floor. He could have used the shaft ladder, but it would be good to know if the elevator worked.

He was happy to see it did. He took the lift from the fourth to the third floor. The door swished open, revealing the pitch-black hallway. The emergency lighting seemed to be malfunctioning here. He adjusted the light on the end of the PDT and pointed it down the hallway. As he stepped forward, the silence grew thicker. He could barely hear the hum of the ship's impulse engines, and not a single system appeared to be active on this floor. The lack of white noise made the hallway feel like a black hole.

Bob slowly made his way to the escape pods.

He pushed open the hold's door. As the PDT's light panned across them, he could see all the pods were still there—every single one of them still in place. Nothing had been triggered, and there wasn't evidence of violence here. This was the one place on the ship that looked to be in perfect order, aside from the fact that there wasn't any power on this floor. He continued towards the Mess Hall area and the Galley.

Standing at the Galley door, he shined the light inside. The door was twisted open. The hinges bent. There had been a contained explosion here.

Gas fire? Maybe that's why the power is out.

He looked inside and followed the revealing light of the PDT across an array of dishes and pots scattered everywhere on the floor. The light threw crazy shadows up on the far wall that danced as he panned across the room. Then, clearly visible just beyond the kitchen workstation were the legs of yet another body, this one in a light gray ship's uniform with a white stripe on the pants, the cook.

Who was the cook?

Bob tried hard but couldn't remember the cook's name. He couldn't even remember his face. He came around the corner of the kitchen counter for a better look, expecting to have his memory jogged and remember the cook's name. Instead, he saw the man, almost comically pin cushioned with an assortment of kitchen utensils. It took him a second to register that the body was also headless, and a nearby rusted-looking cleaver punctuated that story. The light trailed off the body and up towards a large pot on the stove; a splash across the back wall of the stove showed that this was where the fatal blow had happened.

He made his way around the body. His eye caught something inside the tall pot. Apparently, the cook had been making a meal when he'd been attacked. The flashlight lit up the interior of the pot, revealing a disgusting layer of mold and scum mixed with the hair of the cook's severed head, now the soup's main ingredient. Bob couldn't bring himself to get close enough to investigate further; it didn't really matter anyway. He turned around and hurried out of the room, trying not to disturb the remains on the floor.

He knew if he made his way to the maintenance level and the security hub on the second floor, he could check all the ship's systems and see if someone else was still in stasis.

Bob raced down the hallway toward the ascension ladder and pulled himself up and onto the 2nd floor. The lighting here was back to emergency power red. He jogged down the hallway, an urgency in each step as he closed in on a flickering light that stood outside the maintenance section. He was immediately assaulted by the smell of burned circuits and…

The maintenance door whooshed open. Bob stepped back in horror and dropped the PDT. It hit the floor, and its light projected upwards, spotlighting the crucified form of a man. His arms bolted into place, spread-eagled across the main console. A well-used PS-40 bolt gun on the floor. This body was also horribly burned from electrocution as the metal bolts had pierced the console's power conduits. The eyes were savagely torn out of this body, and the mouth had been cut deep into a fiendish rictus of a smile.

Bob closed his eyes, the image already seared into his mind. He turned away and slowly opened his eyes again. The room was smashed, most of the redundant systems broken, torn cables hung haphazardly out of consoles. Circuit board chunks dangled from colored masses of spaghetti wires.

Then he noticed, again, something written in blood, this time, on the floor.

THE DiRecTive IS CLeaR!

It was clear someone had gone cabin crazy. Sometimes people would just lose it; there had been a few reported murders over the years, not unlike anywhere else. People were just sometimes broken, and when broken people were pushed, they would short-circuit like a bad piece of machinery. But this was something far beyond anything he had ever heard of, except for one thing.

In 2182, there had been a Santo-Corp Mining ship tunneling for Rhodium on a Dwarf Planet called Ceres-7. Something had come in from one of the Miners' exosuits, a microbe from a mysterious element they'd discovered. It had gotten into the ship's air and contaminated it. It had been so minuscule that it went right through the filtration system without being detected and infected most of the crew members within 48 hours. One by one, they started to attack each other, acting on rash impulses, reality and logic thrown away, like possessed demons with only pain and destruction on their minds. They did unspeakable things to each other.

Until there was one left.

The final survivor walked into an airlock without an exosuit.

That was almost twenty years ago. Since then, the tech was able to catch the microbes of the deadly element, Nueroxium, and filter them away. Even the PDTs were trained to flag traces, as well as any other foreign bodies. He tapped a few screens and checked the air quality again…green. There was nothing here save for the carbon in the air.

Am I the only one left?

A mild panic started to settle in as he realized he'd now found half of the crew brutally murdered. There were two areas on the ship where hypersleep pods were located. Maybe someone else had gone into hyper; maybe they would know what was going on.

Bob made his way down the hallway, the sense of being possibly alone closing in around him, his peripheral vision starting to play tricks. Approaching every corner or open door, he felt as if someone was ready to attack him, but there was nothing there. Again, he held up the PDT to see if it would register any other crew members, but the screen was blank save for *his* location pinging active. He rounded the corridor and came directly to the security lock-up.

The door here had been welded shut. Someone didn't want anyone to have access. He knew there were weapons in there; it was generally only for cases where pirates would attack supply ships. This had been only on very rare occasions, but it had happened a few times enough to at least warrant its necessity on a ship.

Suddenly, the klaxons sounded, the red lights flashed, and the ship's system voice came online across all the loudspeakers. "Warning: collision course. Auto-nav systems collapsing. Manual flight controls enabled."

Bob sprinted towards the bridge ladder leading to the cockpit. His muscles were starting to wake up now. He felt the strength within them as he pulled himself up the ladder, practically two rungs at a time, and into the cockpit, where he immediately stumbled over a corpse on the floor and crashed headlong into the corner of the Ships Nav System.

Pain stung him like a bright flash. Warm blood trickled down his face. He shrugged it off and jumped into the pilot seat, blinking away the blood in his eyes. The control handles had been broken off, but he could still manage to maneuver what was left of the flight stick. With a slap of his hand, he collapsed engines one and two and went hard reverse on three and four. They powered up from impulse to full reverse in a matter of three keystrokes. He was thrown forward hard against the controls, banging his ribs on the control board. He flicked open a monitor, acting on pure adrenaline-fueled muscle memory. The ship was entering a large asteroid belt.

The klaxons continued with their urgency, as the red lights flashed their warning.

Tiny bits of rock pattered the hull of the ship, knocking systems into a warning frenzy. He pulled hard on the remains of the stick and managed to just graze a sizeable chunk that would have certainly ripped open the side of the vessel had he not maneuvered. The gargantuan space rock passed in front of the monitor with a groaning screech, scraping along the hull.

The ship spun hard to the left. A panel flipped open, and a broken circuit sparked out near his head. He furiously tripped systems and pounded out a sequence on the pilot's keyboard, purging the pulse engines to vent gases from the bow thrusters sideways against the asteroid. The mass continued its destructive graze. Warning lights lit up across the board, indicating minor damage in the ship's systems across decks 2 and 3. A breach in deck two auto-sealed. He counteracted with full reverse on engines one and two. Backing the ship off further until the groaning stopped. He breathed in relief.

He checked the map and started to pull away from the asteroid belt. The NAV system blinked with an odd message:

Virus uploaded:
Systems control Omega Prime.
Special order 7734
Clone redaction model 8 –
System purge status–unresolved, redirect
navigation corrections noted.

Bob stared at the monitor. Confused. The clock showed this message had come in four weeks earlier. The NAV map was current with the plotted course leading them on an auto-corrected route to a Santo-Corp security station near Jupiter. Arrival 3 weeks, 2 days, 13 hours, and 7 minutes.

This wasn't right.

They were under Paulson Systems company orders. Santos was their main competitor. Someone had gained access to the system and uploaded a virus, but he knew he could set a course for a Paulson Systems weigh station as an emergency reroute. A voice behind him spoke.

"That was good, 808."

Bob spun the chair around just in time to see a familiar face swinging an engineering jack at his head.

The hunk of metal landed with a solid blow, striking Bob hard across the jaw, breaking teeth. He could taste blood and feel tiny shards of bone dance along his tongue.

He held up his arms to block the second blow and kicked out with his foot into the midsection of his attacker, driving him backwards. Bob grabbed a small fire extinguisher from under the pilot's station and blasted the attacker in his face. The white powder created a horrifying mask of madness as the man came in for another attack. Bob kicked out with both feet.

Still clutching the jack, the assailant stumbled back and dropped through the ladder shaft to the deck below with a crunch. Bob slid down the ladder after him. He viciously attacked the prone man with an animalistic need to destroy. He didn't know he had it in him.

It was like a switch had been flipped, and he was barely cognizant of what he was doing. He just knew he was fighting for survival. He picked up the dropped jack and smashed it down on the man's right leg as his attacker tried in vain to crawl away. Bob advanced on him like a mad dog.

The maintenance jack making a continual arc of violence, rising and falling...

...a spatter of red accompanying each destructive blow.

Standing over the man, he raised the broken jack but paused. Its face was pulped beyond recognition. Bob glanced at his lifeless attacker's name tag: 807.

The dented, gore-covered jack fell to the deck with a heavy clang. He looked at his own blood-drenched hands and arms, horrified at his actions. His head swam with confusion, and he felt sick. An overload of information poured in.

He slammed into the wall, stumbling down the hallway towards a lavatory. He pushed open the door. The harsh white light blinked and buzzed on with a flicker. He moved towards the sink, and in the mirror he found himself face to face with the person he had just killed.

His vision turned red as the *new directive* became clear:

DESTROY THE 800 SERIES CLONE.

He smashed the mirror and picked up a shard. He couldn't stop his own hand as he drew it deeply across his throat in a vicious sawing action.

808 collapsed against the sink in jets of blood and slid onto his back, staring at the ceiling. This time, a tide of darkness slowly dragged him back out into the ocean of inky black nothing.

The monitor on the bridge blinked an update:

> *Special order:*
> *7734 Clone Redaction model 800 Series*
> *System virus status – Completed –*
> *Redirect ship navigation to Santo-Corp*
> *Security Station 426*
> *for delivery of Triton 6 fuel rods.*

THE EATERS BAND

A STAGECOACH CLAN ADVENTURE

KC GRIFANT

SPACE HORRORS

THE EATERS BAND

KC GRIFANT

I SAVOR WHAT MARY JOKINGLY refers to as "the last meal" in the ship's quiet dining area—tomato bisque beneath floating, soppy cracker bits.

We always joke, with the slightest undertone of seriousness, what we'd have for our last meals before we took off on the mail route. I always go with the same. Tomato soup has been soothing humanity for centuries, after all.

Through the spaceship's observatory deck window, the whirl of stars abruptly disappears as the Eaters Band comes into view—a ring of space darker than the rest and riddled with asteroids. And the mysterious, animal-like Eaters.

"You always pick the most boring meal," Mary says pointing her fork at my soup. For today's mission, she favored a protein flank steak and mashed potatoes, a frequent choice during our last year of working together.

I point my own spoon back at her dish. "Look who's talking."

The Eaters Band gradually grows in the window, showing us just a fraction of the three-mile-thick stretch of space that extended in a steady arc. Beyond the Eaters Band lay human colonies in what we call the "Other Side." That region contrasts with our "First Side," home of humanity's origins. Problem was, while humans had successfully crossed that band to find lush Earth-like planets, transmitted signals could not, requiring unique courier systems to share any information between the two sides.

Without speaking, we both take our last mouthfuls and stand.

"Ready, Mary?" Mary asks, pulling her cloth cap lower on her head to cover her dark curls.

"Ready, Mary," I reply.

The Eaters Band inexplicably fades at random intervals, often several years apart, and that's when ships and all manner of non-human material—tools, supplies—can pass through unharmed. But in between those fades, the Eaters destroy anything non-human that tries to pass.

Satellites. Ships. Convoys. Even micro-flash drives and bundles of paper.

Anything, that is, unless it's in close proximity to living human flesh.

No one knows why the Eaters demonstrate this strange preference—or even how to circumvent it. People have tried sending comms strapped to animals, plants, sophisticated robots. They even strapped equipment to human cadavers. But the Eaters destroy it all. Something about the unique physiology of living humans is the only thing the Eaters tolerate passing through (if those humans could avoid the treacherous asteroids). The working theory is that the complex electromagnetic activity of our brains stops the Eaters from attacking, but whether that's due to curiosity, respect for advanced life, or fear of retaliation is unclear.

Fear, most likely, of a predator that could think and fight back if provoked.

"Approximately seven hours across. No unusual readings," Mary says as we walk, scanning through her notes on a screen projected across her forearm. "But we'll duplicate data on both of us, in case anything gets damaged."

I nod in agreement. "A wise precaution."

Last month, something had gone wrong. A courier in only a spacesuit and air tank made it through the Eaters Band from the Other Side with a message. By the time he reached First Side he was dead, battered by asteroids, spacesuit shredded, and flash drive destroyed. Only a hasty message gave us a clue, one he scrawled in blood on the front of his suit: "Respir. virus killing all, stopping hearts."

The First Side has records of a similar sickness—and how to combat it. Tens of thousands could be saved if the medical information could be passed from one side to the other. Without a fade, couriers can't take a ship. They have to maneuver through the dangerous asteroids only in a suit and with minimal support systems.

That's where we come in.

A few people nod to us reverently as we walk down the worn hall, heading to the ship's departures bank. A mail courier may not have been well respected too long ago, but nowadays it's one of the most dangerous — and lucrative — jobs. There are a few of us elite couriers that have been well trained in all matters of survival, called to deal with any challenging—or bizarre—situations that threaten communications. Reliable information exchanges are core components of a functional, advancing society, after all.

"Timely and Accurate Comms." That's our motto.

We are the Marys.

In the empty departures bank, we get dressed. Mary hums, pulling on the thin suit and boots. I smooth my ponytail back and go through my usual ritual of mentally thanking the others who have braved dangerous courier routes for hundreds of years before us—in particular our namesake, Mary Fields, also known as Stagecoach Mary, who earned the star route contract for the delivery of U.S. mail in Montana, Earth, across the American Old West. She reliably delivered mail across treacherous terrain, despite the threat of wild animals and criminals.

Some 800 years later, Mary and I have gone through the training and had the necessary procedures for enhanced vision, faster muscle reflexes—the works. Now, we pepper our skins with sticky microchips containing AI software that will best glean the structure of the new virus, along with other essential information, all packed into the exact size hardware that seem to be permissible to the Eaters—if near human flesh. We wear the most basic of space suits with minimal technology, our largest device the oxygen tanks on our backs and mini thruster jets on either side of our arms. Our air supply can last as long as seven hours if we don't exert ourselves too much. Once suited, a smaller pod zips us from the ship to the edge of the Eaters Band and releases us, two pale specks against the vast black.

We move slowly, arching our backs with arms down to gently blast the red-orange flames from our thrusters when we need them. We ease out of the way of floating asteroids. The rusty brown rocks are the only specks of color aside from our gray suits. Trouble starts almost immediately as the Eaters move in.

They hang onto the asteroids, waiting. They camouflage with light rather than color, and their forms are fluid. A little larger than an adult human, the closest Earth-like thing they resemble is part octopus and part tardigrade. They appear as blinding white outlines against the red rocks for an instant, before turning to inky black shadows. Somehow, they've homed in on us. We fire our thrusters in the opposite direction for a moment, slowing our movement as not to scare them.

"They're everywhere!" Mary says through the radio as glimmers flash around us.

"Stay calm," I reply. She's greener than I am but well trained. Tension or nervousness makes her voice higher than normal. I spot an obsidian mass with eight long, whipping arms a few feet away from me before it flashes to white, but I don't react. They won't attack us unless we threaten them.

Nonetheless, they attack.

They nip at our shoulders and backs, trying to tear our spacesuits with their flicking tentacles that leave sharp, stinging sensations like being pelted by rocks. I freeze for a second, stunned— they've never, in all the records we reviewed, attacked humans.

It only takes me an instant to respond. I lift my arm and turn on the thruster jet full power, blasting toward them. I fire my other thruster in the exact opposite direction, so I don't propel off course.

Mary does the same. The tactic works. The Eaters pull back, retracting their tentacles and condensing themselves into pod-like forms. It looks as if they are retreating into a shell consisting of three segmented hard shells, about half my torso length, with four tentacles evenly spaced on either side. They take on different colors: transparent, then the same rusty red as the rocks around them, then the same gray as our space suits, and then the flecked brown of Mary's eyes.

I note all the details for later documentation before they disappear behind the asteroids.

"What the hell?" Mary says, her already large eyes even wider.

I shake my head with a shrug. There's still a lot we don't know about the Eaters, but we'll log the encounter as soon as we're out. To conserve energy as we float on, I slow my breathing and hope Mary does the same.

Two hours in and we're still going steady. I stay alert but part of my mind drifts to memories. Fragments of my dad before he passed come to me in these silent moments. Though he was never quite able to mask his disappointment as to why I chose a path of delivery rather than science or engineering like my brothers, we had plenty of good moments together before I left home. I tried to share with him the excitement and satisfaction of getting a delivery done and moving onto the next, as well as the unique challenges and obstacles that each job could entail, but he always saw it as mundane work that others could do, that I was wasting my life.

"You can help more people with science or medicine. Even with the arts," he said to me once right before I left to join the Stagecoach Clan. But the camaraderie of the Marys and the intense training that rivaled any military operation was all I hoped it'd be.

I snap out of my musings as Mary signals a few feet ahead of me. Half a dozen Eaters hover, keeping a steady distance as we continue forward. They coalesce and disappear and then reappear in front of us. That's when I see it: The Eaters are flashing in and out of our range of vision in a pattern. They are distinctly turning from white to black in unison at regular intervals.

Spelling out words.

Morse code! I glance at Mary. The Eaters are communicating with humans for the first time.

Mary lifts her arm thruster, and I tap her to stop. We watch their message flash.

No pass. No pass.

I have no idea how they learned Morse code, but I'm not wasting the chance. I quickly signal back, covering and uncovering my helmet's low light beam for the dashes and dots.

Mary shifts uneasily next to me.

No harm to you, I signal, but I'm puzzled. We aren't the first couriers through, so why are they trying to block us? I shudder as I think of the lone courier who arrived on our side battered to death from being pummeled by wayward asteroids. Or so we had thought.

We need to reach other side, please, I signal.

More Eaters congregate. Now maybe fifty flash in unison as they float in front of us, matching our speed. They blink in and out of sight, saying the same message—No pass, no pass.

I signal back: We need to save humans. Many humans. The Eaters abruptly scatter at my last message. Gone, like a hurled rock had sent them running. An enormous black splotch moves in my periphery, and I duck instinctively from what might be an imminent collision with a giant asteroid.

It's not an asteroid. As I try to make sense of what I'm seeing, the entire band of flat blackness shifts. The Eaters are lining up along an invisible line. And my and Mary's forward motion has slowed, as though something is pulling us back.

Mary's voice comes through, just barely: "Big Eater. Huge!"

That's when I see it: the space around us shifts. The Eaters band moves as a singular entity, like proteins within cells, or cells within organs, I think. A massive creature in which the smaller Eaters operate. A murmuration of Eaters.

Mary trembles next to me.

I signal with Morse, hoping whatever this is, this massive Eater, is listening.

Humans are dying by the thousands.

"We welcome deaths," the entity responds, somehow co-opting the radio headpiece. Its words come through garbled and echoey, like static trying to speak.

Mary stares at me in shock. The Eaters are more sophisticated at communicating than we had ever suspected.

"Why?" I ask, switching to verbal communication. Despite my years of training, my heart begins to quicken at the undeniable hostility in its message.

"You disturb us," the Eaters Band says.

"How? Just by passing through?" My heart hammers inside my suit and a hypothesis bubbles to mind. If the entire Eaters Band is a unified entity, our presence could disturb their ecosystem as we move through. Like a kidney stone.

Or, worse, like a knife through flesh.

"I'll make sure no one passes again if that's what it takes," I continue. It's a bluff I hope the Eaters Band can't sense. My mind is still racing to fill in the gaps. The fades—when we're able to pass ships through unharmed—must be when the Eaters Band entity is in stasis, like sleep. "Just let us through this time, please. We have to save them."

"They die," the Eaters Band replies.

"Why didn't you kill us before if we bothered you so much!" Mary cries out. "Why wait until hundreds of thousands of humans are there already?" She shakes her head. "Needless suffering."

"Limited range to stop you," the Eaters Band says. "You go back."

I glance at Mary as she realizes the same thing. The Eaters Band is stuck in this spot. Whatever internal physical laws dominated it—them—restricted the Eaters to this strip of space, reminding me of ocean creatures that only inhabit a certain depth of seawater.

Not only that, the mystery of why the Eaters Band allowed humans to pass clicked in place. Initially, the Eaters hadn't been able to pinpoint us fast enough. Something in our unique physiology allowed us to move undetected, like a cancer evading a body's defense system. But over time, it had learned.

"We won't let all those people die," I say, and the smaller Eaters immediately start to flow forward, like a wave of shadows.

Mary lifts her arm thruster to blast them.

"You overrun. Overgrow. We watch you. We learn," the Eaters Band says. "No more." The way the words are delivered evokes the full force of their hostility. The smaller Eaters condense into a black ball, some forty feet across, heading straight for us.

"All living things want to survive," I say, even as my mind forms a plan, a last-ditch effort to get the medical information across the band. "We didn't know we were harming you."

"No pass." The Eaters Band's voice fades with a feeling of finality. The mass of smaller Eaters is almost on us, flicking angrily as they approach. I disconnect my thrusters and rig them to Mary. I prepare my energy pack to detonate. She realizes what I'm doing and looks aghast.

It's OK. I've trained for this, I want to say, but she reads my eyes and gives me a nod of gratitude as she quickly accepts my plan.

She'll be the one to deliver. I'll be the one to fight.

She puts all the thrusters on full blast, hurtling toward the Other Side. I watch the gray speck of her suit artfully maneuver between the asteroids as I brace for impact.

The Eaters collide and clamber onto me, tentacles flicking and piercing, tearing at my suit. Cold slams into me like icicles stabbing every inch of my skin. I've reached a state of acceptance, which makes the pain easier to bear. I mentally count down as my energy pack glows ever brighter, readying to explode. One thought gives me a spot of warmth to hang onto in the darkness:

I'm saving thousands after all. Dad would be proud.

LONG HAUL TO HEAVEN

ERIC J. GUIGNARD

SPACE HORRORS

LONG HAUL TO HEAVEN

ERIC J. GUIGNARD

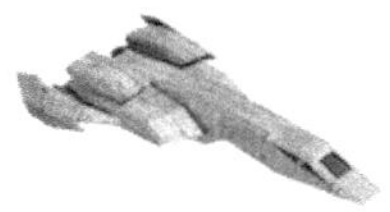

THE DOUBLE BAY DOORS CLOSED shut with two thuds and the hiss from a leaking pneumatic.

Ricky Jack Lisette's torpedoed body came into sight about half a heartbeat later, which was the time it took to clear the upward arching hull of the floating truck stop, LAST CHANCE TERMINUS & SHUTTLE STATION, and into view of the hundred or so humans, aliens, and other amorphic drivers who'd turned out to watch through the thirty-meter-long micro-silicate viewing window.

Ricky Jack didn't look dignified, didn't look peaceful, didn't look nothing but a pale cocoon, just the revenant of a man whom Milky Blue had known and loved for over half his life, now wrapped in a rubberized burial shroud and headed for the oblivion of the cosmos.

Someone muttered, "Scab."

Milky looked around. No one met his gaze. Beside a few looks of mourning that seemed to weigh about as heavy as someone pondering the toothbrush they knocked into the shitter, there wasn't a wet eye in the house.

'Cept for Milky.

Next to him stood half-human Charlie Cash, the only other one who at least gave a salute. Charlie had even dressed decent for the jettison service, although that had more to do with his station, being the Union steward, than anything else; Charlie inclined his head in condolence, and whispered a few words to Milky, and that meant everything. "Ricky Jack was a good man."

"Tell that to the sons-of-bitches who murdered him," Milky said.

"When we find them, I will."

Milky rubbed away a tear that burned so hot down the side of his face he thought it'd surely scar, if scars could layer over other scars.

He stood a foot taller than Charlie and was as sharp-edged and grizzled as the Union steward was soft and unblemished. Milky dressed in black. All black, all the time, from his creased cutter-style cowboy hat to his thruster-soled boots with ebony rhinestones. A faded prison number inked across one forearm and a broken heart across the other. He asked, "That it?"

"Yes, old friend, ceremony's over. Boss'll be calling for shifts in five."

The "service" had been a pre-recorded speech, like something from a tractor shuttle dealer's commercial: *This here man once lived and now he don't, but if he'd bought a Rocket Boost 3000, things might have turned out different.*

Or something like that. There weren't any religious leaders on board, and the Station Captain was locked down in his own drunk tank, so Charlie had to pull a funeral sermon search off the Comm link.

Better than nothing, Milky supposed, though he knew in his heart, Ricky Jack would be cussin' up a storm. Ricky Jack had been to more funerals than Milky could count, many of them *on account* of Ricky Jack, and even if it'd been a mortal enemy to him, Ricky Jack would've been the first to salute their life, respect their rituals.

The other viewers broke up and went their ways, already laughing, already talking about drinks, about the Solar Ball series, about progress— or lack thereof—on the strike.

"Got a minute?" Charlie asked.

"That, my rig, and Patsy here, is about all I got."

Charlie gave the dark-haired female next to Milky a good once-over. Patsy had a hard smile that looked about as cheerful as a cornered jawbeast, but to Milky she was sweet as pie on the inside. A hard life caused a hard countenance was all. Even in repros.

Charlie looked confused but said, "Howdy, ma'am."

"Howdy yourself, darlin'," she answered.

"She's a real doll," he said to Milky, "unless she's a *real doll*?"

Milky gave a short nod. "New A.I. unit I rescued from this slag pit on Festoon 8."

Patsy's laugh belied her true nature, a sweetness that caused the terrible sorrows of her past songs to be so heartbreaking. "I don't know about 'new,' fellas. I've been around a voyage or two, but I appreciate the flattery all the same."

She wore a one-piece flight suit with a white star pattern and suede leather fringe that danced as she moved. On her head was a Stetson hat that doubled as a space helmet at the touch of a button, and around her neck was a jaunty rose kerchief tied at the side. Circling her waist was Milky's arm. He said, "She comes from my part of the universe, this reproduced singer from a few millennia ago. They called her Patsy Cline."

Milky caught the slight scowl, the look of disdain that blew across Charlie's face as fleet as celerity force. *Another droid,* Milky could imagine the other man saying. *Scrap space junk, the lot of 'em, can't be reprogrammed, can't do what a good chip can do ten times over*. Charlie, though, was gracious enough not to say anything out loud; that, or he knew well enough Milky was quick with his fists to defend someone—or some *thing's*—honor.

"Let's take a walk," Charlie said.

"So long as it's in the direction of the taproom."

Patsy fell behind them, and Milky could hear her sing a few soft bars about walkin' after midnight.

They went down a corridor of gray alloy walls and flooring that echoed back each boot step and knuckle crack. Every twenty feet were laser seams and framed photographs of asteroid conquests and, in between, holograms for political advisement or thermo-mechanical advertising.

"I know what you're here for," Charlie said. "And I'm warning against it. You can't go seeking revenge on your own."

"If I hold out for justice, Ricky Jack will be passed over like a high-altitude screamer."

"Even on these outer fringes, we've still got law."

"And you and me both know what that law is worth."

Charlie replied, but his voice didn't match the words. "Times are different."

Milky scoffed. It'd been twenty years since they'd flown freight together in the big-league fleets, him and Charlie and Ricky Jack, back when solar systems weren't so much of lifestyles as they were channels on a transceiver: One day you're flicking through the lush multiplanetary tropics of places like Yibrae 49, then the next you're glazing the overturned icescapes of Puppis White, then after that, star-carping the exotic flesh ports of Libra Libra.

Twenty years now since he'd seen Charlie, though the man was the same, if not for the sagging jowls, the softer gut, the thinning hair: all afflictions from his frailer Human side. He'd always been a hustler, and that's what had got him this station. Milky couldn't guess how long it'd been since Charlie had last flown, since he now just sat behind a desk. Milky couldn't ever imagine grounding himself, no matter the size of the paycheck.

He realized Charlie was saying something, finishing some longwinded contention about why they shouldn't act on Ricky Jack's death. "—and that's why you gotta let this thing rest, Milky."

"Uh huh," Milky muttered.

They arrived at the nested door of The Black Hole taproom, that sort of drinking chamber every galactic truck stop has from here to Aeon 13 that serves rehydrated liquor by the pouch all fifty-eight hours of the day.

Charlie shook his head. "Did you get anything I just said to you?"

"Sure did," Milky said. "Patsy, you roll playback?"

Patsy Cline opened her mouth, but instead of that sweet Southern lilt came the exact recording of Charlie's exasperated pleas. "...there's no exceptions for crossing that line. You were Union once, you know what happens. All it takes is one fracture for the whole wall to breach, and right now we've got the scanners of the galaxy on our negotiations. This'll set a precedent, this—"

"Thanks, Patsy," Milky interrupted. "Think I can gather the rest."

"Milky," Charlie said. "I flew with him too. But Ricky Jack scabbed."

Milky turned hard on his old friend. "You know why, right?"

"Said he was making for Heaven. They're in a tough spot, I know, but that colony brought it on themselves."

"Lemmee guess, you said that same line to him."

Charlie flushed. "Well it's true, bunch of naturalist radicals."

"You Xantju's ass. I'll bet Ricky Jack just shut down after that, didn't he? You remember how he'd get, so upset about something, he wouldn't talk on it no more, just go and split."

"Yeah, ol' Ricky hadn't changed at all these past twenty years. Probably went to go gaze at his daughter's picture in the glow-orb. I remember that treasure lockbox he always kept in the cab, held his important things."

Milky's hands turned to tight fists, but he kept them at his side. "That very daughter is part of the colony."

Charlie's flush turned pale.

"And she just had a baby, Ricky Jack's first grandchild. You should have seen the glow on his face when he talked about that boy. They named the kid after him too, Ricky Jack II."

Charlie gulped hard.

A trio of mean-looking long-haulers passed by, the kind you just knew flew low under cover and came out with armament blasting. The leader was mottled green and purple, with massive biceps on each of his four arms that tested the limits to the elasticity of his aluminized cover shirt.

"You gettin' trouble here, Mr. Cash?" the long-hauler asked. His voice was an electronic translation, coming from the chip underneath his forked tongue. He wore a badge, UNION LOCAL 2896-DEEP. His pinprick eyes bore into Milky.

"No, Thelonius," Charlie said, though he was breathing hard, near to sweatin'. "We're just catching up."

Thelonius made a big show of sniffing in Milky's direction. "Give a call, Mr. Cash, you need us to clear the air for you."

Then they walked past into the smoky din of The Black Hole.

"You want me to correct his course?" Patsy asked.

Milky knew this wasn't the time, not here in the open. "Not yet," he told her, then turned to Charlie. "Should I be worried?"

"Those three are trouble, all right. I got no real authority over them; they're *protected*, if you get my drift. They catch wind you're going up against the Union, those are the first you'll answer to."

"Could they be the ones who murdered Ricky Jack?"

"Could be… could be any number of others on this truck stop, too, though. We got over two thousand on board." Charlie paused, looked at Milky's set expression, and went on. "That big one, Thelonius, he's been flying long haul about a hundred years before you or I was even born. He'll recite labor law to you spit and polish while he rearranges your face. The other two have got major rank as well. The shorter one is Rin Sick, comes from Arabxis Valley off Sky World. No one better with a pair of flesh cleavers. The stocky one with the hydraulic legs and glass faceplate is JJergish. He's got a blaster under his leg port, left side, so be careful."

"Aren't I always?"

Charlie looked around, then glanced inside the taproom. "I'd go in there with you, have a drink or three, but I'm on the clock. Reports to file and shit."

"You're a company man, I get it."

"Listen," Charlie added. "I didn't know about Ricky Jack's family, that they're over there."

Milky leaned in, his voice dropping to a serious whisper. "There's more, if you can help."

"If I can, I will."

"That baby, Ricky Jack II, he's sick in a bad way."

"Hell."

"It's medicine they need, a shipment. Not to mention the food they've been begging for. They're starving down there; the crop generators caught on fire, hydrogen simulators reprogrammed themselves to implode. It's like they're hexed."

"I know what's going on there, Milky, that rock the colony's on is a Union contract. But all our driver pilots are on strike. No one flies delivery off this station until disputes are settled."

"There's no other way to get out there without stopping here first! Even our farthest long-range Chargers can't reach Heaven without refueling, resupplying here."

"I know, Milky, but there's no exceptions. Those colonists are the ones who went out there against advisement from the Survey Council, citing goddamned 'Religious Exclusion'." Thought they could live *the natural way*, communing with the asteroid. Grow their own food? Make their own laws out of jurisdiction? Live off the grid where no one can reach 'em? What were they thinking?"

"I can reach 'em, Charlie, and I'm flyin' out of here tonight, with or without your help. I'm going to deliver Charlie's cargo for him."

"Milky—"

"You never been on Earth have you?" Milky asked.

"No, my father was a human driver, but the bastard took off before I was born. Spent my childhood on my mother's planet, the Argon district of Libra Libra, the underworld tunnels."

"There's this sickness full-blooded humans can get, a disease called cancer."

"Never heard of it."

"It's exclusive to Earth-born, so no one else in the Universe cares. But it kills us faster than anything, our own bodies turning against us. Not even longevity serums work. And Ricky Jack II, he's got a bad one, in the brain."

"Sorry to hear."

"He needs treatment, and there's a holistic medicine that could heal him. It ain't even been synthesized yet, just naturally harvested: venom from western Texas, where me and Ricky Jack hail from. The venom, it's mixed with these nanobots and capsulated to kill the cancerous cells."

"Venom?"

"Comes from a type of bark scorpion, this small animal we got out there, eight-legged, mean, deadly. The venom's invaluable."

"Invaluable, you say?"

"The point ain't profit, jackass, but to heal, it's medicine to the disease. A *natural* medicine, like the colonists believe in."

Charlie sighed. Bit at a fleshy lip and thought. He pulled out a flip-Comm Uni-Set. "I'll see what I can do, you're so dead-set on this. But you call me, Milky, you keep me apprised of where you are, what you're planning to do each step of the way. Here's my code."

"Will do, old friend. And thank you."

***

Milky Blue and Patsy Cline went into The Black Hole. It was noisy and dimly lit, just the emergency lights on, which gave the taproom a bloody red pallor. Driver pilots sat in twos and threes tossin' back liquor pouches, throwing darts, watching OrbitComm reports or Solar Ball on a dozen different screens.

Milky called out to Patsy as he sidled up to the bar, "Anything you want, pretty lady?"

"Just your smile, Milky."

He obliged, which he didn't do much for anyone else, then faced the bar's DrinkTender. Milky stuck out his tongue. A chip glowed, a set of lights blinked, and a scanner peered in his mouth. A pouch emerged off a little lever. Whiskey Double with a dash of peppermint. Just the way he liked it. He stuck out his tongue for a second round.

When he turned back, he saw through the open nested door that Charlie was still out there, just the rear edge of his wide ass and a gesturing hand visible. He was having words with the stocky driver, JJergish. Even with the glass faceplate on, Milky could see JJergish's yellow eyes flick to him and narrow.

Milky moved to a small hover table in the corner, sat close facing Patsy, so their knees brushed. He leaned in. "What do you think?"

"Your friend, Charlie, he's hard to get a read on. But his heart's not true to his words. I've known too many men like him—he's got liar's eyes and a yellow streak to boot."

"Damn, I was afraid of that. He's changed, softened. If it was twenty years ago…"

Milky thought back.

Twenty years ago, they'd been invincible. *Literally.* Hell, longevity serums saw to that, barring any physical calamity. But it was the corruption calamity that brought them down. They were caught transporting illegal goods—weapons, hijacked spice hauls, uncut gemstones. It'd been a set-up. All Milky knew was what the Bill of Lading had said when his rig had been loaded up, listing: *Secure freight, commissioned produce, frozen.* Milky had been Union back then, not even allowed to handle, much less open, any of the shipments. All he'd done was fly the cargo.

Interstellar law didn't see it that way, and justice agents were paid off to send him to hyper lock-up along with Ricky Jack for near a decade, taking the rap for some unknown smuggling operation. Being as Charlie Cash was only half-human, he'd gotten off on a technicality; Milky always thought holding different legal standards to planetary species was bullshit, though he'd never have wished their circumstances on Charlie to share.

So Charlie Cash went on to better things, staying Union, transferring to where you got paid the most, at the longest of long-haul operations on the outskirts of the explored universe, where he rose through the ranks, resolving disputes and carrying out orders from Union strongholds.

When Milky and Ricky Jack got free, they quit Union, went owner-operators, each flying their own long-haul business, but they kept in touch over the years. That's how Milky found out, a message two weeks delayed in Comm Drive that Ricky Jack was coming here, was going to cross the picket line of the bitterest labor dispute in two thousand years of interplanetary labor laws. And then he was killed—

An electronically-translated voice interrupted his thoughts. "Heard you're from Milky Way."

Milky snapped alert while the light darkened above their table, blocked out by a massive figure.

He looked up to the cratered contours of Thelonius's face. Next to him stood Rin Sick, a flesh cleaver hanging off each thorny leg.

Milky's fingers started to tingle, wanting to move. "That's right."

Thelonius snorted, which coming from him sounded like a photon explosion. "Should have known. You're nothing but a bunch of cowboys and roughnecks out there."

Milky grit his teeth. "What do you want?"

"To see what you're made of, maybe."

Now Milky rose from the table, keeping his center of balance low. The rest of the taproom fell quiet, turning to watch. "About two hundred pounds of pissed-off fury."

Thelonius looked surprised for a moment, then wary. "Sounds like what I shit out after breakfast." He backed off a step, crouched, and even then, still towered above Milky. Two of his arms rose high, the other two doubled in.

"You got serious health problems then," Milky countered, circling away from the table, clearing his range.

Someone snickered. Thelonius tensed. "No non-Union drivers come out here. You're a scab, Earthman, I can tell. Just like the other one."

Now Milky tensed. His hands went up, cupped mid-range on either side of his head. *Don't let him get you wild.* He said, "What do you know about Ricky Jack's murder?"

One of Thelonius's arms came around from the side mock-punching at Milky, checking distance. It was like an animal batting at a plaything; Milky didn't flinch. Thelonius had been quick in movement though. Surprisingly. "What everyone else knows."

"And what's that?"

"Wasn't any heartbreak here to see him gone."

And then all hell broke loose. Thelonius took a swing, a straight arm that came flying in at Milky somewhere about the speed of light. Milky had been watching it though; Thelonius had given himself away, using that same arm to check range to 'test' Milky. Milky didn't need to test anyone. He parried the other's open left hand straight up, deflecting Thelonius's fist, then slid his fingers down to lock around his wrist. At the same time, Milky hooked his right arm around Thelonius's trapped limb, took two steps to the left and wrenched apart like cracking loose a stuck combustion bolt. He'd had plenty of years to perfect his moves on ice eaters while in hyper lock-up.

He heard the bone snap. But it didn't stop there…

Thelonius's entire arm broke apart, into two pieces, and Milky was left unexpectedly holding half a forearm and a hand of wriggling fingers. Thelonius screamed and fell back, crashing through chairs and hover tables. Milky did a double take,

80

then threw the appendage the other way in disgust. He barely had time to see Rin Sick make his move, leaping forward, a flesh cleaver spinning in each hand.

But the next moment Rin Sick was blown backward by a stun prod to the chest that left him curled on the floor next to Thelonius. Patsy lifted her trigger finger to her lip and blew away the trail of smoke that circled up from the flex barrel under her red-painted fingernail.

She stood over them. "Darlin', you don't know what heartbreak is till the man you love drives a fist through your teeth and then spits in your eye when he's done."

Thelonius had his eyes closed, moaning, his three remaining arms holding the stump of the missing one. Rin Sick sort of convulsed a few times while his own eyes came back into focus.

"That was my pointer finger," Patsy added. "Don't make me use my middle." She held that one up to them.

Milky advanced. "Which one of you killed Ricky Jack?"

Thelonius cried out. "We didn't do nothing to him, we didn't kill your friend!"

Milky put a boot down on Thelonius's ankle. Pressed on it, hard. Thelonius moaned.

"You won't like if I have to ask again. Which one of you—?"

One of the others in the bar, a reptilian driver with two heads, raised cyborg-spliced hands to Milky. "Easy there, friend. Thelonius is innocent. Same with Rin Sick."

Milky barred his teeth. "How's that?"

"They were flying the picket line when Ricky Jack was shot in the back. I was with 'em, and there's a dozen others here who will attest the same. I'm not saying these two are clean-handed, but they're not responsible for murder."

Milky stepped off Thelonius. "Who then?"

The driver shook each head sadly. "Couldn't tell you. There's flyers in and out of here all day, Union handlers, brokers, inciters. Could have been anyone else, but not these two."

"Hell," Milky said. He curled a lip, rubbed at the stubble on his cheek. Looked down. "I didn't mean for your whole arm to go like that, just a breaking blow was all..."

Thelonius got to his feet, swaying. His electronically-translated voice was a little quieter. "It's okay. Third time it's happened this month. It'll grow back tomorrow."

"Huh," Milky said. He gave a nod of acknowledgement to the long hauler then motioned to Patsy. "Think it's time to go."

He thought to call Charlie's Uni-Set, tell him what had happened, but he saw several other driver pilots in the corner speaking furtively into transmitters, and he got the feeling Charlie already knew.

****

Milky's rig was parked in Bay 314, and they were halfway there when they came to a juncture to turn ninety degrees into the long access corridor branching out for Bays 200–275.

"This way, pretty lady," he said to Patsy, following the turn.

"That's the wrong way, Milky. We're straight ahead."

"It's the right way to figure out who killed Ricky Jack."

She inclined her head but followed Milky's lead.

"Ricky Jack's rig," he said. "It's in Bay 264. It's left as-is, since he was killed. Investigation protocol, for whenever someone gets around to doing such things."

"There's nothing to be found at his ship. Your friend wasn't killed there, he was murdered in a prep room."

"True, but I think word's gotten out that we're gonna follow his intention. That cargo he has, other drivers are finding out it's real important to us."

"I still don't get it, hon."

There was the sound of a distant bay door opening and thrusters firing up. A scrabble of echoing footsteps. The lights in the corridor flickered. He could smell the rich burn of fuel conductors.

Milky slowed the pace. "Whoever wanted to stop Ricky Jack from scabbing, ain't going to let us get that cargo."

"But we already have our own. You got a copy of his Bill of Lading; we duplicated his payload before coming here."

"Hush now, they don't know that."

Patsy nodded, grinning. Her eyes sparkled like the cosmic dust of a supernova. "So we're walking into a trap, Ricky Jack's murderer waiting for us?"

"If this were cards, I'd call that a straight flush probability."

"Well, at least you're not a dull date."

They reached the entrance for Bay 264, and Milky looked up and down the corridor real casually, while Patsy placed her pinkie finger into the access lock and ran an override program. The door opened, and they went in.

The bay was cold, dark but for a row of softly glowing running lights. Even in the gloom Milky recognized Ricky Jack's rig, a tractor shuttle almost as old as his own, each of the eighteen wheeler's wheel wells converted to hold Vertical-Lateral Thrusters the size of asteroids.

Patsy's nostrils flared. She whispered, "Someone's here all right. I can smell nitrogen triiodide."

"Contact explosive..." Milky muttered. He reached inside his flight jacket. His hand came out holding an XM ChatterGun, small and powerful enough to aerate a body but not decompress a room. "How much?"

One of Patsy's eyes rolled up to the white in computation. She froze while sensors measured the air, before replying, "Enough to clear out this hangar."

A whisper came from the shadows, "With you included."

Milky turned in time to catch a Solar Ball bat across the side of his head. His world exploded in a fusillade of pain and twinkling stars, and as he sank to his knees the memory of Ricky Jack Lisette's sad shaking face came before him, as if to say, *You dumb shit, got caught faster than a one-legged hare.*

Milky tried shaking his mind clear, but everything was muddled, slow, and he watched Patsy snap out of her Computation Mode to defend herself, but not in time, as the bat clobbered her too. She fell like a dropped pylon.

It'd been a double play.

Milky still had his gun though, and he lifted it in a wavering arc, trying to regain his balance. A hydraulic leg kicked his hand hard, and the gun went clattering away. His wrist screamed out, feeling like a power thruster used it for a launching pad, but by that kick, at least, he knew who he was up against.

JJergish.

"Give it up, scab." The voice was flat, no inflexion, no emotion at all.

"Like hell," Milky said, and launched himself at the larger alien.

The tackle caught JJergish off guard, and even with his hydraulic legs, Milky managed to knock him down, and they landed in a tangle on the pyrolyzed carbon floor with Milky on top.

Milky angled up his head and brought it down in a vicious head butt, slamming against JJergish's glass faceplate. The faceplate cracked, and the alien's eyes winced in shock. Milky made a hard fist, knuckles out, and punched hard into JJergish's throat. That brought a cry of pain, long and drawn out like an air leak.

The alien tried getting his legs under him, wrenching around beneath Milky, until belting an upward palm strike that caught Milky on the chin.

Milky's teeth clattered, and he rolled to JJergish's left side, remembering the blaster that Charlie had said was kept there in a leg port. He thrust an elbow into the alien's cracked faceplate, drawing a satisfying grunt, while his hand reached into the port for the blaster...what Milky pulled out instead was a ribboned medal reading: UNION

STRONG, PROUD SR. MEMBER OF LOCAL 2896-DEEP, 25 YEARS.

What the hell—

JJergish's free hand wrapped around in a hook punch that connected square with Milky's kidney, and JJergish pushed off him, rolling back the opposite way until springing up into a crouch. His hand went to the port on his other leg—the right—and out came a double shot blaster.

"Looking for this?" he asked.

Milky cursed silently as he rose from the ground on his elbows. He was too far away to do anything but too close to dodge a shot. A blaster like that was going to shellac the whole bay with him no matter what he did. He hawked a wad of spit and blood.

"I didn't want to leave any photon residue on you," JJergish said. "Wanted to blow you to Parthinian Hell with this rig, make it look like an accident, but no matter. I'll just jettison the lot of you. Won't be nothing left to investigate anyway."

So this is how it's going to end, Milky thought. *It wasn't the worst way, even if he'd failed…*

JJergish laughed, a sound—like his voice—without inflexion, without emotion, as if dry tapping a wrench on a drum head. "You might've lived if you'd stayed Union."

"Say, nickel-legs," came the sweet Southern lilt of a voice.

JJergish turned in time to see Patsy Cline point her middle finger at him.

"I promised myself long ago, I wouldn't let no man ever hit me again and get away with it." Then a red light shot out with half the sound of a breaking sound barrier and twice the speed, and JJergish exploded in a cloud of alien blood, armor, and hydraulic bits.

Patsy lifted her middle finger to her lips and blew away the trail of light particles circling up from the flex barrel under her red-painted fingernail.

She helped Milky to his feet, and he grimaced as he leaned into her. "Thanks, pretty lady."

"Any time, darlin'."

"We better get out of here, that bomb's still set."

They did, and just as the bay door closed behind, there was a tremendous explosion from within.

"You satisfied?" Patsy asked. "Got your friend's killer?"

"I'm about halfway there," Milky admitted. "But he wasn't alone in this. We're gonna have to revisit later though—that explosion will draw others."

"Time to fly out?"

"Yup, and fast. The only advantage we got is that whoever else is in on this will think we're nothin' but space muck, blown up with Ricky Jack's rig." He listened for a moment to alarms blaring, voices yelling, running footsteps drawing near. "As soon as they find out we're still around, it may well be every driver here after us."

"Not much of an advantage at all," she said.

Milky lifted a thumb up to the dropped ceiling. "Duct work. Ain't the first time I've escaped that way." He crouched down, held his hands together in a lift-step. "Ladies first."

He hoisted Patsy up, and the partition dividers lifted easily aside. She went in, then helped pull Milky up. They set the dividers back in place and crawled along the metal framework by Patsy's flashlight eyes until they'd come back above the corridor where Milky guessed his bay, 314, should be.

They dropped down quietly into the hallway, and Milky saw he'd been near dead-to-reckoning. They were in front of 313. They walked over to the next bay in line and entered through its door.

"Almost too easy," he admitted.

"Sometimes the good luck comes your way to balance out the crap," she replied.

"About time."

Patsy ran her fingers gently across the back of his hand. "Take it, Milky, and wager for more."

He gave her a smile that seemed to stretch back millennia, to touch the ghost of a heart wanting nothing more, and she returned it to a long-haulin' man of the future who thought he could never make another being happy.

"Let's get haulin'," he said.

Milky's tractor shuttle was a Peterbilt Space-5500, about thirty years old, though it showed those years tenfold. Milky liked to say that if her dents could talk, your ears would give out before you got to the fifth vacuum coupling.

The cab was gunmetal gray, smashed in on every corner with more scratches and dings than a flame rock shower. The windshield was splattered by grit and astro bugs, the fenders scorched by char, the chrome was chipped and dull, the grill filled with meteorites. The mud flaps showed matching silhouettes of a cowgirl lazily tossing a fishing pole.

She was resplendent, and she pulled a double-hitched 53-foot-long trailer topped by articulated rudder fins. Like Ricky Jack's rig, all of Milky's eighteen Vertical-Lateral Thrusters had been modified for maximum fusion-driven flight.

Milky and Patsy boarded, he in the driver's seat, she in the gunner's. They fired her up.

"As soon as the outer bay doors open," Milky said, "they're gonna know we're leaving."

"What then?"

"Hopefully we'll outrun anyone who scrambles fast enough to give chase. As soon as we landed here, I ordered our deuterium and tritium fuel pellets refilled and, see by the gauge there, we're set. Enough to make Heaven, and then make it back, at least, to whatever awaits."

"Lock-up?" Patsy asked.

"No," Milky chuckled. "Probably worse. But I wouldn't worry that purty head of yours yet; let's just get out of here quick as possible, get the supplies, the medicine, to Ricky Jack II. That's what matters."

"I'm with you, Milky, all the way," she said, and placed a hand over his on the Solar Ball knob top of the long-barred gear shift. "Fingers crossed we get past with none the wiser."

"Lady's luck." Milky winked at her, then activated the outer double bay doors to open.

They flew out into space…

…and Milky cursed three times. Patsy groaned. She said, "Sorry, darlin', my luck has always been crap."

Extending across the expanse of the rig's windshield hovered a line of tractor shuttles, all wingtip to wingtip, and all facing them. Each one had rockets, warheads, blasters, therma-guns, and everything else pointed at Milky.

The picket line. They'd set up, just for him, with over a hundred craft, if he guessed.

The primary Comm Drive video screen flashed on in his cab. The image of Thelonius faced him, buckled into his own driver's seat, probably a Mack Astro-3200XX rig, Milky figured. That was the tractor shuttle in the center lead of the line, about a kilometer away.

"You've got ten stellar-secs to return to that bay you just left," Thelonius said in his electronically-translated voice, "otherwise we'll send you back there in pieces."

"You have no authority over me," Milky replied. "I ain't Union, and I got a delivery to run."

"But I *do* have the authority, Earthman. I represent the Intergalactic Trade Organization, and Stellar-Covenant 145 on Economic Rights expresses our right to strike in unfair labor conditions."

Milky rolled his eyes. Put his rig into neutral. "You have the right to strike all you want, and I have the right to cross your line. And *that* is in Convention Clause 18c, which permits the unrestricted freedom of non-Union drivers to fly without interruption or fear of reprisal."

Thelonius shook his head. "Each signatory galaxy of the Covenant has right to abridge Clause 18c, and here in Quadrant Ph3, strikebreaking has been ruled prohibited as detrimental to outerworld collective bargaining."

"The hell it has," Milky said, though his voice was unsure. He glanced at Patsy.

"Afraid that's true, darlin'," she whispered. "I'm scrolling through Labor Law now.

We're in a Union security-protected sector, and they can stop or impede strikebreakers by whatever means necessary."

"But not murder?" Milky said questioningly.

Patsy made a face. "Ricky Jack?"

Milky turned back to the Comm Drive video screen, speaking to Thelonius. "We're going through that line, asshole."

Thelonius pointed the stump of his broken arm at Milky. It had already begun to regrow. "Just try it, scab, and you'll be going to one different type of Heaven!"

Milky shook his head once, looked straight into the screen unblinking while he increased the throttle to maximum power, getting ready to charge.

Patsy placed a hand on his shoulder. "Milky, I'm with you, but we just ain't no match."

"Ten," Thelonius said.

Milky unclenched his jaw, took a breath, looked at her honest eyes.

"Nine," Thelonius said.

"All right," Milky said to Patsy. "Guess, I got one card left." He switched on the small transmitter for his personal Comm Uni-Set. Keyed in Charlie Cash's code.

"Eight."

"Hold your prick and panties," Milky told him. "I'm calling your boss."

Thelonius snorted, that sound again like a photon explosion. "Who, Charlie? He may be the Union paper pusher, but out here on flight paths, *I'm* the boss."

Charlie's face appeared on Milky's Comm Uni-Set. He sat behind a desk overloaded with paper folders and file cabinets like the battle spires of a crumbling fortress. "Milky, that you?"

"Yeah, I'm in a situation."

"I heard. You done it now, old friend."

"Seven."

"Great, you can count," Milky shot back. He said to Charlie. "We on a secure line?"

"That's what Uni-Sets are for, encrypted one-on-one."

"Call off your pack," Milky said.

"Six."

"No can do. I warned you." Charlie leaned away, showing a lockbox in his lap, with his thumb on the latch.

"The hell!" Milky shouted. "Is that… that Ricky Jack's lockbox?"

"No point letting it go with the rest of his rig."

"You son of a bitch, you knew to pull that treasure box before blowing his rig—You're the one killed him, ain't you?!"

"Five," Thelonius said.

"It wasn't me who shot him, it was JJergish." Charlie closed an eye, thought for a moment. "But I did order it, so yeah, I guess that sort of makes me responsible."

Milky suddenly had to blink too many times. "I guessed it, I knew it, but I didn't want to believe.

You're the one sent JJergish after me too. You even tried throwing me off, telling me he had a blaster on the wrong leg to put me at a disadvantage. Ordered Ricky Jack's rig blown up, set the picket line against me. You chose Union over friends, over the life of a child!"

"Four."

"Aw, hell with the Union, Milky. You think that's all I'm about? They pay fine enough, but I make my money through smuggling, spices and gems shuttled to every port in the universe aboard freight shipments. It's the loaders who are paid off, and driver pilots don't even know. I've been at it for twenty years. The Nebula Brothers got me infiltrated into the Union in the first place, back when we flew together, just to do this."

"You damned yellow crock of piss, it was you who me and Ricky Jack went to hyper lock-up for!"

"Three," Thelonius said. Milky flipped a finger at the long hauler via the primary Comm Drive screen.

"Sorry, buddy," Charlie said. "It wasn't meant to have gone down like that, I was still learning the ropes, the finesse of it back then, you know."

"So what's that got to do now with Heaven? There're no freight deliveries out there, no ports to fence stolen goods. The colony's alone out in the ass-end of space!"

"Two."

"Funny thing, Milky. There's the richest ore deposit of Coronal Energy Stones ever found, and it's located right on Heaven. I've got smugglers going out there every other day under cover to mine it. They're the ones who sabotaged things for the colonists in the first place, setting fire to the crop generators, reprogramming the hydrogen simulators, just trying to get those naturalist radicals to uproot. Sorry as hell to hear about Ricky Jack's kin being part of it, but, you know, them's the breaks. Can't have any uninvolved drivers going out there, stumble upon what we're doing, so it's all the more reason to extend the strike."

"One," Thelonius said.

"Give me five more!" Milky roared at Thelonius. "Five more stellar-secs! I'm gonna back out."

"That won't do you any good," Charlie told him. He lifted Ricky Jack's treasure lockbox to his ear. Shook it back and forth. There was a clatter and rattle of things inside.

"Five," Thelonius said.

"Hell, it'd probably be easier on you to just let them blast you out there in space," Charlie said. "Less painful. Otherwise, you'll get it in the back like Ricky Jack, if you return here. We'll call it 'resisting detention.' Pretty fitting, since you're a known convict and the such."

"You had it planned all along," Milky muttered. "But Ricky Jack ain't that stupid."

"Four."

"Naw, he wasn't," Charlie agreed. "But being as he's driftin' the long flow to nihility, it don't matter, does it?"

"The venom, you know, the medicine needed to cure his grandson?"

"Three."

"I told you it ain't synthesized, just naturally harvested," Milky said. "There's only one way to do that."

"You always could bore a dak-yak to tears, Milky. What's your point?"

"Two."

Charlie flicked up the lockbox latch. Dumped out the contents on the desk.

"My point is about what's inside of that," Milky said. "It's live specimens."

Charlie screamed, long and loud and horribly. Milky's last view of him before the Comm Uni-Set cut out, were the bark scorpions pouring out of the box, starved for weeks and frenzied, falling onto Charlie sitting in the chair.

"One," Thelonius said. "Prepare to engage."

The weapons of the picket line armada began to glow, track, and load.

"I already died once," Patsy said, clutching the armrests of her vinyl seat. "I don't want to again!"

"Thelonius," Milky said. "I got a message for you."

"What's that?"

"Patsy, roll playback."

Patsy Cline opened her mouth and out came the exact recording of Milky and Charlie's conversation, all the way up to his screams: "*…hell with the Union, Milky. You think that's all I'm about? They pay fine enough, but I make my money through smuggling, spices and gems shuttled to every port in the universe aboard freight shipments…*"

Thelonius listened the entire time, motionless. But the green and purple mottling of his face turned redder and redder at each word, until he looked like a radiating hypergiant sun set to explode. He uttered some tooth-clenched command Milky couldn't understand, but the weapons on the other tractor shuttles all powered down at once.

"Charlie Cash," Thelonius said in his electronically-translated voice, "is hereby revoked and further banned from Union membership. And I've got a long-range nuke launch for his farewell."

"Permission to cross your line?" Milky asked.

"Granted, Earthman. I believe this strike is over."

The primary Comm Drive video screen flashed off, and Thelonius's Mack Astro-3200XX rig pulled away. The other spacecraft followed.

"Heaven, it's a long way still," Patsy said.

"It is, pretty lady, and I don't wanna hear no more blues singing on the way out there, got that? Just happy songs."

"I recall one or two of those, but this might be time to pen a new one," she said and placed a hand back over his on the Solar Ball knob top of the long-barred gear shift.

Together they put it into drive. She said, "Think I'm gonna call it, *Milky's Smile*."

He gave her one, and she returned it, and the stars sparkled around them, and a comet shot past, and off they flew, makin' a long haul to Heaven.

SPACE HORRORS

LUCY'S WRATH

KATHRYN BLANCHE

SPACE HORRORS

LUCY'S WRATH

KATHRYN BLANCHE

"MAYDAY, MAYDAY, MAYDAY! Does anyone read me? We are under attack! The experiment failed—OH, DEAR GOD! SOMEBODY HELP!" The woman's scream was cut off as the transmission ended.

My stomach dropped as I watched the ghost ship we were approaching. "When was that from?"

"Three days ago. Considering that there are no responses to our attempts to hail the ship, I doubt there are survivors." Lieutenant Ramirez frowned at his tablet.

"Why the delay?" asked Chief Petty Officer Marti, his second in command.

"We were the closest team available with the resources needed to conduct the search. The ship is registered to a Biotech company—probably a lab. The mission is to assess what happened and report back. Dr. Sheffield will accompany us."

Lieutenant Ramirez turned to me. "Go prepare the doctor."

"Yes, sir!" I saluted, then started towards the door.

"And Petty Officer First Class Kelley—"

I paused and glanced at the lieutenant.

"Keep an eye on him. He's used to the lab, not life out here."

I nodded before leaving.

***

Down one of the far corridors, I spotted the doctor near the door to his lab.

"Dr. Sheffield, we need you for a mission—" I stopped and watched the scientist shuffle about, hunched over by the door. "Doctor?"

He glanced up at me sheepishly, and I could see the cord of his credentials caught in the lab's door. "Oh! Hey Vanessa—um, First Class… Officer Kelley? So sorry! Do you think you could, um—" He gestured to the scanner.

I swiped my creds, and the door released him. He sighed with relief.

"Thank you so much, Vanessa!"

I chuckled and shook my head. "You have got to stop doing stuff like this. If one of the others catches you trapping yourself in a door, you'll never hear the end of it."

"I know! I know! It's just… I'm not used to being on a ship." He gestured to the spaceship surrounding us. "It's a little nerve-wracking. You know, the lack of air outside."

"Well, you don't need the new Petty Officers giving you a hard time."

I followed him into the lab. He had hundreds of plant specimens for transport to Europa, and it felt so lush in the lab compared to the rest of the ship. A digital photo frame rested on his desk, a photo of a little girl giving the camera a toothy grin, her hands moving as she signed a message.

"Cute kid. Is she your daughter?"

"No, my niece. She was so excited when she heard I'd be going to Europa. She loves space. She wants to travel on a spaceship someday." He cringed as if saying the word 'space' was becoming a trigger. I hoped he would be able to handle this new mission.

"Well, we need you to get suited up. We've got a mission."

The color drained from his face. "What? Out there?"

I briefed him as we hurried through the corridors and towards the airlock. As we reached the equipment room, the poor scientist looked like he was going to be sick. The rest of the team was already getting into their spacesuits.

The doctor hesitated as a soldier waved him over to his waiting suit. "So, we're going outside?"

"Hopefully not, but you never know." Petty Officer Jackson smirked and winked. He and most of the others were new to this ship. Judging by his youth and cocky attitude, he had little experience out here on the frontier.

I shot him a look. The team members ranked below me and technically answered to me, as I was a petty officer first class. Lieutenant Ramirez, however, would be taking point on this mission. "It's part of the protocol for boarding derelict ships. Just in case they're unstable or contain contaminants."

"But, one thing to be aware of, Doc, is that our comms will be limited in range," Lieutenant Ramirez explained to the scientist. "We're not connected to the other ship's network. If too many walls separate us, we won't hear you. The walls of these ships are just too thick. It limits contact with our ship, too. So, stick close, okay?"

The scientist looked uneasy but allowed two petty officers to help him into the suit. I donned my own and wondered if we should bring Dr. Sheffield at all. This felt like a lot to expect of a man who dedicated his life to studying plants, but it was not my place to question orders.

"You okay, Kelley?" asked the lieutenant, too low for the others to hear.

I shrugged. "Sometimes, I wonder what it would be like to head back to one of the bases on Earth or Mars. I could get a house and a dog and not have to deal with derelict ships, pirates, or desperate scavengers."

He double-checked my suit. "I've told you it's an option. You could transfer. Hell, you could become a civilian. Have a normal life."

He moved along to check Dr. Sheffield, leaving me alone with my thoughts. Perhaps it was time to leave space.

"Ready?" asked Lieutenant Ramirez.

"Yes, sir," we chorused.

"Move out. Stay frosty. We don't know what happened or what dangers are onboard."

As a group, we headed toward the airlock. The doors shut behind me with a hiss. I felt a twinge of apprehension, remembering the last ghost ship I boarded and how I nearly got sucked out into space after an airlock malfunction. Dr. Sheffield was right to be concerned. I took a deep breath and followed the lieutenant as the doors to the ship opened.

"Any idea what the lab on this ship was used for?" asked the scientist.

"That's what you're here for, Doc," Petty Officer Carson sneered.

I shot Carson a look, and his grin grew wider, but he kept his mouth shut.

Hiss!

It sounded like a door, but no one was supposed to be alive. My eyes narrowed, searching the corridor. Someone gasped over the coms.

The lieutenant made eye contact and nodded. With a sharp incline of my head, I proceeded to where this corridor intersected another. The lieutenant inched towards one corner while I took the other. On his cue, I glanced around the corner, and my stomach lurched.

"All clear!" called the lieutenant.

"We've got three civilians down!" I called.

The lieutenant swore and started barking orders to the others.

The first body was slumped against the wall. I forced my lunch back down as I stared at his face— or what would have been his face. Most of it had been ripped away, leaving the pale white of his skull to peer through muscles and tendons. His throat had been ripped out as well. A quick glance at the rest of the body revealed that his innards were beginning to turn to soup. The other two were in similar condition.

"Shit. What would have done this?" asked Carlisle, examining the wounds. He was a petty officer first class like me and had been with us for several months now. He only seemed mildly disturbed, unlike the new petty officers who hung back. Jackson looked ready to puke in his helmet, a harsh shift from his earlier display of bravado. To my surprise, the doctor was only slightly disturbed as he joined Carlisle. What would desensitize a botanist to such carnage?

Dr. Sheffield shook his head. "Your guess is as good as mine. I'm a botanist, not a coroner."

On the lieutenant's orders, I proceeded down the corridor. We needed answers. Given this ship belonged to some biotech company, it seemed like the lab was the best place to start. I took another step as the lights started to flicker.

"We'd better get to the computers before the power shuts down," I said over the comms.

"Kelley's right. It should be down the corridor to the left. It's the first door on the right. Carson and Carlisle, cover our flanks."

We hurried down the hall, ensuring the corridors and doorways were clear. There were more bodies, each appearing to have been mauled. On Earth, I had seen attacks by wild cats and wolves, but these were different.

I reached the corner at the end of the corridor and paused. I quickly peered around, gun at the ready, but the space was deserted. Not even a body in sight, just the locked door to the lab.

We inched forward, watching for any sign of movement. Carlisle pulled out a tablet and hooked it up to the card reader on the lab's door.

"I'm not sure about this," whispered Dr. Sheffield as he took a step closer to me.

"Easy, Doc. The sooner we find out what happened, the sooner we can get out."

Click!

Dr. Sheffield flinched, but it was only the lab door opening. I grabbed the doctor's arm, motioning for him to wait while the others cleared the room.

"Clear!" called Jackson.

I nodded for the doctor to enter and then followed, leaving Carson and another new petty officer, Smith, to guard the door.

The lab would have been sleek and sterile with bright white finishes and stainless-steel lab tables and equipment, but instruments and broken glass littered the floor in pools of mystery chemicals. I was glad we were still wearing our suits and helmets. A woman's body lay in a puddle tinted red with her blood. This time, I could make out stab wounds on her body. Was that less concerning or more?

Beyond a thick pane of glass, along the far end of the room, there appeared to be some sort of cell or observation chamber. It was filled with a child-sized table and chairs, a jungle gym, and a scattered assortment of toys and books.

"What sort of sick bastards experiment on children?" spat the lieutenant.

My stomach churned. "I suppose that's why they were way out here."

I turned away from the enclosure. Sometimes it was hard to tell if things were better or worse now that space had opened up as an accessible frontier. Sure, there were new planets and moons to explore and terraform. But there was just so much space. It was a bit too vast and a bit too easy to get away with unspeakable crimes.

The lieutenant pointed to a sign on the window that read *Lucy*. "We've only seen adults so far. Perhaps Lucy is alive and managed to hide somewhere?"

"Maybe? But that's a lot of carnage." It seemed like wishful thinking at this point.

Dr. Sheffield joined Carlisle at the computers. Within moments, he overrode the security features and started sorting through the files.

Dr. Sheffield frowned. "There's so many files."

"We'll copy them to sort through later. We just need to figure out what happened before we leave. There're several entries from the last day." Carlisle opened the first, which was an audio file. It was a woman's voice:

"7:06 UTC on September 9th, 2231. As usual, we gave Lucy her morning rations. She seemed oddly quiet and withdrawn, or more so than she had been lately. She also had little interest in her food."

"8:32 UTC on September 9th, 2231. Lucy is still withdrawn. She has not touched her food. We attempted to coax her into doing some arithmetic problems, but she refused. This asocial behavior is unusual. I am beginning to suspect she is feeling unwell."

"9:12 UTC on September 9th, 2231. I noticed Lucy lying in the corner of her enclosure. I've tried speaking to her through the microphone, but she does not move. We will prepare to examine her to ensure she is not in distress."

I avoided looking at the cell. Although there was a marked shift in tone indicating some level of concern, the callous notes were nauseating.

"Something's wrong! Lucy's attacked the technicians. It's premeditated she's—" A blood-curdling scream tore through the recording. "She—she's got a knife. Run! Run—" There was more screaming and sounds of pleading through the commotion. Then nothing. The recording continued in silence.

"I-I don't know whether to be shocked or relieved that the little girl ended these experiments," stammered Dr. Sheffield, and he closed the file.

The lieutenant scanned the room once more. "I wouldn't be so sure. Even if this is a little girl, she's killed a ship full of people. We don't know what sorts of experiments they did, but it's safe to assume she's dangerous."

A distant clanking noise echoed through the corridor. I exchanged a glance with the lieutenant.

"Kelley and Carlisle, stay with the scientist and copy the files. Jackson and Carson, you take the left. Smith, you're with me," ordered the lieutenant.

The others split up. I kept watch in the doorway while Carlisle and Dr. Sheffield finished downloading the files onto a tablet. Minutes ticked by painfully as I strained to hear the others.

Their voices on the coms cut out, and there were no sounds down the corridor. Quiet should be good. It meant they had not found anything yet. But that wasn't as reassuring as it should be for some reason.

"Almost there," said Carlisle.

"Um, Vanessa," started Dr. Sheffield.

"Yes, Doctor?"

"I think you may want to—"

A distant scream echoed down the corridor. Shots were fired. I thought it was on my left.

"Let's move!" I barked.

Carlisle unplugged the tablet, shoved it into the Doctor's hands, and drew his firearm as I rushed toward the sounds of conflict.

"Vanessa! Wait! There's more!"

I hurried down the corridor, stamping down the fear and settling into cool focus.

"Vanessa, this experiment. It had to do with intelligence," Dr. Sheffield said. "This drug they were using caused mental capacity to triple in weeks. Over years of study, that could mean we're dealing with a remarkable level of intelligence."

"Let's just focus on surviving first, Doc. Data later."

We neared a corner, and I motioned for silence. I glanced at Carlisle before looking around the corner—

"Shit!"

I aimed at the blur that shot past me. I was about to open fire when it registered that it was Jackson scrambling away. I turned back, expecting the girl to be in pursuit, but there was nothing, aside from a couple of corpses dressed in lab coats.

"All clear." I turned to Jackson. "What is going on?"

"It attacked Carson! It ambushed us and stabbed him from behind. I tried to get it off him, but it stabbed him in the throat." The words tumbled out of his mouth.

What kind of a girl can take down a soldier like that? Something was off, but I had to get to the others. This was the girl's territory, and she knew it better than we did.

Dr. Sheffield grabbed my arm. "That's what I'm talking about—"

I shook him off. "I know there was probably a lot in the file, but we need to find the others. If she's vanished, she may try to go after them too."

I sprinted down the corridor, the others keeping pace.

"Lieutenant Ramirez, respond if you can hear me."

114

Nothing.

"Lieutenant?"

"The walls are interfering," said Carlisle.

We rushed past the lab, following a bend in the corridor.

"Lieutenant?" I tried again.

"Vanessa? What's going on?"

Hearing his voice, relief washed over me. "Carson is down. The girl killed him."

The lieutenant swore. I finally saw the others emerge from a doorway further down the corridor.

"It's not a girl!" cried the doctor.

"What?" the lieutenant and I chorused over the coms.

The ship shuddered as flames exploded through the doorway behind the lieutenant and Smith.

"No!" I screamed as the force of the blast knocked me off my feet.

Then there was darkness.

***

Something was dragging me forward. I struggled blindly, searching for a handhold. Was it the girl? No, not a girl. Not according to Dr. Sheffield. Then what was it?

I stopped moving. Had it dropped me? I switched on the light on my helmet and scrambled to my feet. Dr. Sheffield, Jackson, and Carlisle lay in a heap behind me but seemed unharmed. Lieutenant Ramirez was slow to move, his hands still grasping the handrail along the wall. Beyond him, a pressure patch pulsed a faint orange, covering the hole where the door had once been. I checked it, and the mechanical patch seemed secure, but the hole was easily three times the size of a doorway. We needed to get out of this wing and shut the airlock before the pressure patch failed.

"Are you okay?" I helped the lieutenant up. His suit had been damaged on the right side. His sleeve burned clear through, and his skin badly scorched.

I eyed the wound. "We need to get you back to the ship."

"Where's Smith?"

I looked around, but there was no sign of him.

"Smith?" I called. No response. "Smith, come in!"

Carlisle limped over. "He's gone. He was sucked out in the blast."

This was not how this mission was supposed to go.

"We need to fall back," ordered the lieutenant.

We nodded and headed for our ship. I stopped long enough to verify that, although Dr. Sheffield was a little banged up, he could walk.

"Come on, we need to get off this ship."

He seemed a bit dazed but nodded.

"Do you think she rigged those explosives?" asked Jackson, watching our backs as I guided the doctor forward.

"P-possibly," said the scientist. "There was speculation in the notes that Lucy knew more than she let on, but it was hard to tell because she's not human."

"What do you mean, not human?" I glanced over my shoulder but couldn't make out any shapes in the beams of our flashlights.

"What the hell?" grunted Lieutenant Ramirez.

I nearly stumbled into him as he stopped short. Down the corridor in front of us stood a small, hunched figure covered in stringy hair. The chimpanzee stood eerily still.

"That's Lucy," whispered the scientist.

We raised our weapons.

"Wait!" cried Dr. Sheffield. "Don't attack! She's intelligent."

"So what?" spat Jackson.

"So, she can be reasoned with."

The doctor had a point. And she was between us and our ship. We might outnumber her, but if she was smart enough to rig some improvised explosive, then who knew what other traps she had set.

The lieutenant gave me a look that told me I would be handling this. I slowly set my weapon down and I put my hands up. I avoided eye contact since I recalled some animals found it threatening, but I kept my focus on her. The chimpanzee watched me warily. Her hand tightened around a large kitchen knife. Her fingers were bloodied, and dried blood matted the hair around her chin.

"Do you understand me?" I said over my suit's speaker.

She gave me a defiant look and bared her teeth. I felt Jackson tense.

"Please, I need you to tell me if you can understand me."

The chimp nodded hesitantly.

"Can you talk?"

She shook her head and gestured.

"Is that sign language?" asked the lieutenant.

"Yes," said the scientist.

"Can you understand her?" I recalled his niece signing to him in that video message.

"Yeah, mostly."

"What happened here?" I asked Lucy the chimp.

She signed something, and Dr. Sheffield translated: "The doctors in the white jackets hurt me. They were nice to me sometimes, but they hurt me. They changed me. Made me different—smarter. I wanted to go away, but I was trapped. Nowhere to go. Stuck. I knew they would hurt me again and again, so I made a plan to stop them."

"Did you kill them, Lucy?"

"Yes. I didn't mean to. I got angry. I was afraid they would hurt me. So, I stopped them. I stopped them all from hurting me." Her features softened, and her eyes grew wide. I saw fear and uncertainty.

"Is that why you tried to kill us? You thought we would hurt you?"

She nodded.

I motioned for the others to lower their weapons. Reluctantly, they did so.

"Lucy, we don't want to hurt you. We just came here to see what happened. We needed to report what those people did to you—that they hurt you. We need to make sure that others don't try to hurt anyone. Does that sound okay?"

She nodded.

"Can you put the knife down?"

She paused a moment but did as I asked. I stayed wary, though. Chimps were strong, and I knew she could rip my face off without a weapon. Still, it signaled cooperation.

"If you stay here, you will die. There are not enough resources for you here."

"I know," translated Dr. Sheffield.

"If you come with us, we can take you somewhere safe—somewhere you will be treated with respect. You can tell the authorities about how the others hurt you. You will have to be locked away for now for everyone's safety, but it will only be for a little while. What do you say? Will you come with us?"

The chimp thought it over. "You will not hurt me?"

"Not unless you hurt us."

The others hardly dared to move. Seeing the extent of her ability to communicate was a bit unnerving. It confirmed our suspicions about her intelligence. If she had more explosives, she could kill us all. We needed to be careful to avoid angering Lucy.

"What am I?" Lucy asked at last.

The question caught me off guard, but she continued.

"I am not a human, but I'm not an animal. I don't know what I am."

"Why is that important?"

"Because I am alone. Even if I go with you, I am alone. All I wanted was to not feel pain, but what now? What good will it do?"

"What do you mean? You can help stop this from happening to others. So, you're one of a kind. Why should that stop you? Everyone feels alone sometimes. Hell, I feel alone sometimes, especially out here. But out here, I have a purpose: to protect people. I help ensure that our future is safer."

Lucy pondered this for a moment, and just when I was convinced she would say no, she nodded. "I will go with you."

I breathed a sigh of relief. "Good, now let's get off this ship."

Lucy walked with us. Jackson watched her like a hawk. It was hard to blame him for it; after all, she killed two of his friends. I felt uncertain myself. But leaving her to die felt wrong. None of this was her choice. Although experiments had been banned on primates long ago, it seemed even worse in this context. Lucy may not be human, but she was close.

Yet, at the same time, Lucy also had the ability to kill. That could not be overlooked. She might be as unpredictable as she was intelligent. Then again, humans were the same. They showed me that time and time again. The destruction Lucy wrought was disturbing, but I had seen humans do far worse both on and off the battlefield. So, what did that make us?

We returned to our ship, recovering Carson's body as we went. We would try to search for Smith's once we separated from the ghost ship.

"You're all clear to disconnect," said the lieutenant over the ship's coms once the airlock shut behind us.

Our ship disconnected and backed away from the ghostship. Scanning for Smith, but Chief Petty Officer Martin found nothing.

"There might not be anything left to find if he was close to the blast," our second in command said over the coms as she backed us away from the wreckage.

We silently changed out of our spacesuits while Lucy waited and watched. Jackson wandered off in a daze. The lieutenant gave Carlisle and Dr. Sheffield orders to get Lucy settled in a spare room. I sat on a bench and nodded to them as they started to leave.

Dr. Sheffield froze, narrowing his eyes at the ghostship through the window, "What's that—?"

There was a brief flash of light before our ship lurched forward. I toppled off the bench as the others were thrown off their feet. The lieutenant bellowed as he fell on his injured arm.

I glanced up to see Lucy grinning, her eyes watching me with an empty, haunted expression. She signed something.

"Dr. Sheffield?"

"She said: Finished."

Dr. Sheffield and Carlisle shook themselves out of their shock and led Lucy down the corridor, trying their best to ignore what had just occurred.

I helped the lieutenant to his feet, and we watched their retreating forms.

"What did we get ourselves into now?" muttered the lieutenant.

"I want to think that was just a final act of defiance—one last way to get back at her captors, but…" I trailed off.

The lieutenant raised an eyebrow, waiting.

I grimaced, "But I can't help but think we could be next. Do you think she's smarter than us?"

"Would an ordinary civilian figure out how to rig a ship with explosives? One with a timer that could be set without us knowing about it?"

That was a good point.

The lieutenant continued. "We'll chart the fastest course to Europa and hand her over to the authorities and the lawyers. They can figure out what to do with her."

"Let's just hope we make it to Europa."

He watched me for a moment. "You know I'm serious. You've been in the service for over ten years now. This doesn't have to be your life."

I thought about it for a moment, watching the debris floating in the distance. "I know, but like I told Lucy, out here, I have a purpose. And you need all the help you can get."

He gave me a look that said he could manage, but I ignored him.

"Now, come on, lieutenant, let's get you to the medical bay. Then we can figure out what we can do about our unexpected passenger."

Lucy was alone and terrified. She fought to protect herself from those who harmed her. Was it justified? Probably. At least, I knew I would most. Likely do the same if I was captured and tortured.

We were supposed to be out here preventing harm, but it was an uphill battle. Biotech companies like this one were just the tip of the iceberg. Theoretically, any field or industry seeking to avoid regulation by any government could be hiding out here doing God knows what. Crime and violence felt like the currency of this frontier.

I could not turn my back on this job, not if I wanted to be able to look myself in the eye every morning. I may not have the ability to stop all these criminal operations, but there was one thing I could do: I could do my best to protect the people who dared to venture forth into space to build better worlds. I could protect those farmers, scientists, and engineers who were taking that leap of faith to ensure there were safe planets and moons to support life for generations to come.

VINCENT V. CAVA

SPACE HORRORS

FIRST CUMTACT

VINCENT V. CAVA

ANOTHER CAVE.

Another stupid, goddamn cave.

The darkness had crept in like a steady tide as the expedition party made their descent. Now, two kilometers deep, they were drowning in it. Flashlights offered little help. Golden beams sliced through the pitch-black, hinting at fantastic mineral formations, but visibility remained limited. What the three astronauts could see was incredible, nonetheless.

Enormous, glassy pillars sprouted from the floor, some as large as telephone poles. Translucent stalactites hung from the ceiling, crisscrossing this way and that, like the great, jagged teeth of a giant.

Crystal vines meandered down rocky walls, and glistening gemstones peeked up from the dirt. On Earth, such a place would be considered one of the Natural Wonders of the World, but on X-35A, a small planet three hundred and fifty thousand lightyears from the solar system man called home, it was just another cave.

Captain Harker was beginning to worry about the morale of his team. This was the sixteenth underground cavern they'd surveyed since their ship landed on X-35A earlier that week, and so far, each and every one had been nearly identical. The planet might have been a geologist's wet dream, but his crew hadn't crossed the cosmos to look at rocks. He knew that if their fortunes didn't change soon, they'd be forced to report back to command empty-handed.

The captain cleared his throat and prepared to give the other two men yet another pep talk.

"Remember why we're here," he said. "The deep space observatory's findings suggested this is the most habitable planet our astronomers have ever discovered. Yes, it's true the surface is a barren wasteland with windstorms powerful enough to blow your skin clean off your skeleton, and the atmosphere is composed of toxic, lung-melting gas, but according to the bio-markers we've detected, there's a good possibility these caves are harboring the building blocks of life! We can't stop until we find it!"

"Stop!"

The shout came from the team's biologist, Dr. Edward Ball. He was crouched over a hefty boulder, leaning so close to the rock that the helmet of his spacesuit was almost kissing it. Harker rushed to his crewmate's side and aimed a flashlight over his shoulder. The beam caught a crystal embedded in the wall and fragmented into a thousand unruly rays. He grimaced at the sudden blinding flash, then adjusted his electric torch in the direction of Ball's gaze. Once his eyes could focus on what had captured the biologist's attention, his head began to spin.

"Is that what I think it is?" he asked.

Growing out of a crack in the boulder was a small patch of pale, white mushrooms. Ball retrieved his bio-scanner and started waving it frantically over the discovery.

"Biological markers are similar to simple fungi found back on Earth." He smiled up to the captain. "We've done it. We've found life, sir."

"Get a sample," said Harker. "We'll take that back to the deep space observatory when we dock there to refuel. This is it. We're going to be in the history books, gentlemen."

The biologist slid a pair of scissors from his pocket and pruned a mushroom at the base of its stalk. He held it up proudly for the other crewmates to see.

"Since it's my discovery, I guess I get to name it."

"Sounds fair," agreed the captain.

"Gentlemen," said Ball. "Allow me to present to you definitive proof that life isn't exclusive to Earth. A finding that will change how we view ourselves, the universe, even God. I give you the ball fungus."

"We can work on the name later," the captain said.

"Whoopty freaking do," groaned a voice behind them.

Harker and Ball spun around and shined their flashlights at the third member of their crew. Lieutenant Lori was leaning against a massive slab of quartz, arms folded across his chest. He squinted back at them through the window of his helmet and pouted.

"Is there a problem?" the captain asked.

Lori sighed. "No. Yes. It's just that Ball gets the alien fungus named after him, and I don't."

"It's only fair!" Ball cried. "I found it!"

"Right. And I get that, but Harker said we're all going to be in the history books, and I can't help but feel like I'm going to be a footnote."

Harker raised an eyebrow.

"Lt. Lori, you are among the first men to step foot on the only other planet in the galaxy that we know harbors life."

"*Among the first.* Way to sugarcoat it," Lori said. He was getting annoyed. "I was the second person to step foot on the planet. Not the first."

"And that matters how?" the captain asked.

Lori shook his head. "Neal Armstrong. That's a name people know. Your average idiot doesn't care about the second guy on the moon. Hell, you're an astronaut. Can you even name the second guy on Mars? No? Didn't think so. It was Mitch Kowalczky. And it's not like I learned that in school. The only reason I could tell you his name was because it was an answer in a game of Trivial Pursuit my neighbors broke out last month before a swinger party."

"None of that matters," Harker said. "This trumps every other accomplishment in aerospace history."

"You were at a swinger party last month?" Ball asked.

Lori scoffed. "Oh, please! You know people are too lazy to learn more than one name."

"I have more faith in humanity than you do," Harker said.

"Which neighbors?" said Ball. "I live down the street from you. Why didn't I get an invite?"

"Besides, this is about more than personal glory," growled the captain. "This is about advancing science! It's about learning mankind's place in the universe!"

"Captain Harker was the first one off the ship," Ball said.

Harker clicked his tongue.

"So?"

"So," Lori laughed derisively. "That means you get to be in the history books, and I'm just the answer to a Trivial Pursuit question collecting dust in Buck and Sheila Crockett's board game closet!"

"Sheila Crockett? She's on the HOA," Ball said. "Hey, can you get her to ease off about my bushes?"

"Who cares, Lori?" Harker groaned.

The lieutenant jabbed a thumb into his chest.

"I care! At least Ball has his ball fungus."

"We haven't locked that name in yet," said the captain.

"I signed up for this mission to make history. Not to be known as number two! Do you know what I think of number two?"

"Shit!" cried Ball.

"Exactly!" Lori said.

"No. I mean, shit! What the hell is that?!"

Ball pointed a trembling finger towards the far corner of the cave. Even shrouded in the darkness, the three men could tell they weren't alone. Whatever was in there with them was the size of a small car and it was moving. The eerie shape lurched forward, and when it did, a horrible pop filled the cave. Harker swallowed a scream, not wanting to appear weak in front of the rest of the crew. Slowly, he lowered his flashlight and washed away the shadows that had been hiding the hulking mass.

The creature's skin was transparent. A mapwork of deep purple veins spread out across its robust, tube-shaped body. It had no head or even a face. In fact, it was impossible to tell where the beast ended or began. Grotesque, pink craters were scattered along the thing's frame. They bubbled occasionally, inflating and deflating like slimy balloons. Growing from the top of it were six tentacle-like appendages. They waved about in the air as if beckoning the men towards it.

"Incredible!" Ball said. "I can't believe it! Complex alien life!"

The men moved closer to get a better look but stayed on guard in case the creature was dangerous. Ball pointed his bio-scanner at the lifeform and began to study its vitals. Another pop broke the silence, and everyone jumped. The astronauts lowered their flashlights towards the creature's feet, which looked like large pink suction cups. They noticed both they and the lifeform were now standing on a large patch of the mushrooms Ball had discovered. The ugly thing lowered its suction cup foot on top of some mushrooms. As it did this, the bubbling craters in its skin began to pulsate more intensely. They swelled and glowed for a few uneasy moments, then let out a deep, thunderous belch. There was a pop when the lifeform lifted its foot again, and the men could see the mushrooms beneath it had vanished.

"It's grazing," Ball said. "It uses those suckers to sustain itself on ball fungus."

When the thing burped again, a notification chimed on Harker's wrist monitor. The screen lit up. He checked it, studied the readings, then studied them again just to be sure he wasn't imagining what he was seeing.

"I don't believe it," he said. "The air is breathable."

Another belch boomed from the slick, slimy openings in the creature's body, this one longer and wetter than the last. Ball placed his hands on his hips and began to ponder.

"It's possible that the gas this lifeform is producing is dissipating the toxic chemicals in the air around us, leaving only oxygen."

Harker flipped the latches of his helmet.

"What are you doing?" asked Lori.

The captain lifted the helmet off his head and took in a deep breath. The other two men stared in awe. Harker smiled.

"It's safe to breathe, guys."

Ball and Lori followed the captain's lead and removed their own helmets. The captain grinned at Lori.

"Complex alien life that produces breathable air. How's that for your history books?" he asked.

Lori shrugged. "I don't know. It's pretty amazing. It's just..."

"Oh, what is it this time?"

"Ball was the first to see the lifeform, so he'll get the credit."

"I was?" asked Ball.

"Yeah, when you pointed at it and said, 'What the hell is that?'"

"You're right! Looks like I get to name this thing too." He gazed down once again to the creature's peculiar, cup-shaped feet and watched it consume more mushrooms. "Gentlemen, may I present to you the first complex, extraterrestrial lifeform humanity has ever discovered. The ball sucker!"

Lori frowned.

"Congrats, Ball. You and Harker have solidified your places in history. I was just kind of there."

"My communicator doesn't get reception down here," Harker said. "We need to report these findings back to the deep space observatory pronto, but I can't get ahold of anyone."

"Figures," whined Lori.

"What figures?"

"You're just changing the subject because you know you're going to be famous when you get back to Earth and nobody is going to care about me."

Harker exhaled a quick breath of alien cave air from his nose. "Alright, Lori. You want to be the first so bad? Why don't I just tell everyone you were the first on the planet or say you discovered the lifeform? Happy?"

"That's not fair!" Ball stamped his foot. "I discovered it! You can't just take my ball sucker from me!"

"No deal!" Lori said. "I'll know it was a lie, and I won't be able to enjoy my fame!"

"So what the hell do you want to do?" grunted the captain. "Because you're obviously not going to shut the hell up about this until you get to be the first at something."

Lori turned his flashlight back on the creature. The men were silent for what felt like eons as they watched him consider the captain's question. Only burbles and gurgles from the lifeform's digestive tract filled the dark void they were standing in. Finally, after a particularly loud belch, Lori returned his gaze to the captain. His eyes were sharp. His face solemn. Both Ball and Harker knew he had come to a decision.

"I'm going to fuck it."

"I'm sorry, what?" said Harker.

"I'm going to fuck the alien," repeated Lori.

"It's a ball sucker," corrected Ball.

"I'm not expecting foreplay, but I wouldn't turn it down."

Harker ran a hand through his hair as he attempted to make sense of what Lori was suggesting. Eventually, he gave up. "Why?" he asked.

"Because no one else has!" cried Lori. "I'll be the first documented person in all of human history to have sex with an alien from another planet. Now, there's something for the history books!"

The captain narrowed his eyes at his lieutenant.

"I don't think they'll teach about that in school."

"Maybe in sex-ed."

Harker tilted his head. "You're not fucking the alien."

"Why not?"

"A million reasons!" he shouted.

"You could fuck a jellyfish," Ball said.

Lori stared dumbfounded at the biologist. "A jellyfish?"

"If you really wanted to fuck something no human has ever fucked, you didn't need to travel three hundred and fifty thousand light years to do it. You could have just stayed on Earth and fucked a jellyfish."

Lori huffed. "Look me dead in the eye and tell me you're sure that in the entire history of the human race, nobody's ever come across a jellyfish washed up on the beach and thought: *Gee, I wonder what it would feel like if I put my dick in it?*" he said.

Ball scratched at his chin. "You make a good point."

Lori began to move towards the alien, but Harker stepped in front of him.

"Hang on," said the captain. "It's not like this is some green-skinned, three-breasted bimbo. How could you even be attracted to it?"

The creature belched again, a scent similar to sulphur wafted up the nostrils of all three men. The holes in its body were oozing a clear slimy substance, and its veins were throbbing, emitting a deep purple glow.

Lori scrunched his face.

"You think I'm attracted to that thing? I'm not some pervert! I just want to be the first to fuck it for science or something! Now, out of my way!"

Lori unzipped his pants and pulled out his manhood. He hawked a loogie in his palm and began to crank away in preparation.

"Wait!" the captain said. Harker was still standing his ground, although he was finding it increasingly difficult, considering his lieutenant was shaking hands with his soldier just two feet in front of him.

"It isn't ethical!" he finally blurted out. "The alien can't even consent."

"Incorrect, Captain Harker." The voice that replied was smooth and soothing. It did not belong to any of the men in the cave. "I consent."

Flashlight beams darted all over the cave as the crew searched for the source of the voice. It wasn't until the flashlights fell back on the creature that all three men came to the simultaneous realization that the words they had just heard had somehow been projected inside their heads. They glanced at each other to confirm, then back to the alien lifeform.

"Did the ball sucker just speak?" Ball asked.

"Affirmative," answered the voice again. "I am a sentient species. I can ponder my own existence. And I do consent to sexual intercourse with Lieutenant Brad Lori of Earth."

"Good enough for me," Lori said. He spit in his hand again.

"Hold it!" Harker said. "Isn't it good enough that you spoke to it? You are the first person to communicate with an alien."

Ball raised a finger in the air. "Technically, Captain, the ball sucker was answering you when you questioned its ability to consent to sex with Lori, so that would make you the first person to communicate with an alien species."

"Doctor Ball is correct," the alien responded. "I was addressing the captain."

"For Christ's sake!" cried Lori. "You two keep racking up firsts. Now I *have* to fuck the alien."

"How are you speaking with us?" asked Harker in an attempt to steer the conversation away from interspecies sexual relations.

The creature's tentacles began to wave about again. The strange craters in its skin resumed pulsating. It let out another couple sulphur-scented belches before answering.

"My species communicates telepathically. By reading your mind, I analyzed your language—English—and have become fluent in it."

"Sure, why not," shrugged Ball.

"I'm going to fuck it," Lori said.

"I forbid you," commanded the captain. "And put your johnson back in your space suit!"

"You're jealous, aren't you?" grinned Lori. "You're mad that when we get back, people aren't going to even care who stepped foot on this planet first or what the hell ball fungus is. All the watercooler talk is going to be 'Hey, did you hear that Lori porked an alien?'"

"A little cynical, don't you think?" Harker said.

Lori shook his head. "It's not cynical. It's realistic. We're a stupid, horny, sex-obsessed species. Insert a penis into anything, and it becomes all people care about. I can see the news headlines now. *'ASTRONAUT HAS SEX WITH EXTRA-TERRESTRIAL SPECIES. Sexual act takes place on newly discovered habitable planet, but honestly who gives a shit? You're reading for the alien fucking.'*"

"He's right," Ball said. "Captain, I think I want to fuck the alien too."

"You can't be serious," sighed Harker.

"You can get in line after me," Lori said. "I'm going to fuck it first. They'll probably call it a lori sucker when I'm done with it."

Ball shoved Lori. "No way. The first guy to fuck that thing makes history. The second guy is just some weirdo."

"You may copulate with me too, Dr. Ball," said the alien.

Ball unzipped his spacesuit, spit into his hand, then began to pump his member.

"I said I'm going to be the first!" shouted Lori.

He dropped his flashlight and lunged at Ball. The two began to wrestle. Chests grinding and swords clashing, they grappled in the darkness.

"What are you two doing?!" shouted Harker.

"Making history!" the other men shouted back.

The captain tried to slide between his crewmates to break up the fight but caught a fist to the chin for his trouble. He hit the ground and lost his own flashlight. When he tried to get back to his feet, he stumbled. The punch had left him disoriented. In the shadows he could hear the other men's battle rage on.

"Stop it, you idiots!" he called out to the darkness.

But Ball and Lori wouldn't listen. The scientific expedition had devolved into chaos. Grunts and curse words echoed in the cave. The thud of fists pounding flesh filled his ears. Just when he thought the fighting would never end, there was a sudden crash, a loud scream, and then all was silent again.

Harker found his flashlight and got back to his feet. He turned it in the direction of where the clamor had been, then gasped. Ball was on the ground, a puddle of blood pooling around his head. Lori was standing over him, teeth clenched and hands balled into fists.

The captain scrambled towards his downed crewmate to check his vitals, but once he got a good look at the biologist, he knew that wouldn't be necessary. Ball's eyes had rolled up in his head. His face was as white as a ghost. Embedded in the back of his skull was a large piece of crystal that had been sticking out of the cave's floor.

Harker glared up towards his lieutenant.

"What have you done?" he shouted.

"It wasn't on purpose! He tripped!"

"Help me take his body back to the ship," the captain sneered. "We're getting out of here. Lori, I will be reporting you to the astronaut core. I'll see you face charges for this!"

"Fine! Do that!" Lori said. "But first, I'm going to fuck that alien!"

"Are you kidding me?" Harker was incensed. "We just had a crewmate die, and you still want to stick your junk in that thing? For what? So you can be known as the universe's biggest pervert?"

The alien remained quiet, aside from the occasional belch, of course.

"I don't care what they call me," Lori said. "I trained for years to make a name for myself, and I'm not going to let it fade into obscurity."

Harker had heard enough. If Lori wasn't going to listen to reason, maybe violence would do the trick.

"Zip up your damn pants right now, you jackass!"

He landed a punch that sent Lori onto his ass. Harker looked down, scowling at the lieutenant. He was furious and disgusted with the man but also a little impressed that he'd managed to maintain his erection.

Lori wiped some blood from his lip with the sleeve of his spacesuit.

"I see what you're doing," he growled. There was a crazed look in his eyes. "You're trying to get me to go back to the ship so you can lock the doors then run back here and fuck the alien yourself!"

"You're paranoid," the captain said.

"You get it," laughed Lori. "You get that nobody is going to care about you and what you did here once they find out I stuck my dick in that gassy, slimy meat-sack!"

"Listen to yourself, Lori," said Harker. "You're talking madness."

The lieutenant palmed a jagged, softball-sized crystal, broke it off a rock, then staggered to his feet. He shuffled towards Harker.

"You want all the glory for yourself," he said. "Well, not on my watch!"

Lori swung the crystal, bludgeoning Harker in the face. The commander dropped his flashlight once again and fell back to the ground. The rock had made him loopier than the fist had. If he could see through the darkness, he was sure the cave would be spinning. He felt Lori mount him. Harker tried to fight back, but his arms were heavy, and he was struggling to breathe with the lieutenant sitting on his chest. There was a second bash from the rock, and he knew his teeth had shattered. He tried to beg for mercy between blows, but the words couldn't form fast enough to escape his mouth.

"It's mine!" screamed Lori as the captain's blood splattered against his face. "I'm going to fuck the alien! Not you!"

After a few minutes, Lori dropped the rock and rolled off Harker's body. He lay panting on the ground as his rage dwindled. Command would have questions about Ball and Harker when he got back, but that didn't matter. They didn't matter. They were just afterthoughts, bit players of his epic story. All he had to do was complete his mission. Make history.

Lori pawed at the ground until he found a flashlight, then illuminated the creature once more.

"There you are," he said.

He cranked at his shaft as he lumbered towards the lifeform.

"Are you ready?" he asked.

"As they say on Earth, give it to me, big boy."

***

Commander Paulson was a strong, burly man, which is why he had no trouble shoving aside subordinates who had gathered around the deep space observatory's docking bay. The ship they'd been expecting from X-35A was four days late but had finally arrived just as he had sat down for dinner. He hadn't eaten at all during his twelve-hour shift, so he was hangry as hell, which is why he did find some pleasure in jabbing his elbow into crewmembers as he pushed through the crowd to greet the expedition team.

As he neared the front of the group, it became increasingly obvious that the buzz amongst the men and women around him was not one of excitement, but concern, and once he reached the entrance hatch, he understood why. Lori was on a stretcher and being treated by medical staff. His body looked emaciated. His eyes had dark rings around them, his cheeks were sunken, and his arms and legs were rail thin.

"Damnit!" shouted Paulson at no one in particular. "This man looks like hell! Get him to the medical bay immediately!"

The crew began to scramble around him. One of the medical staff positioned themselves behind Lori's stretcher and started rolling him away.

"It's good…to see you…Commander," Lori said.

Paulson reached out and grabbed the stretcher, stopping it in its tracks. He gazed down at Lori who was smiling back at him. Even though he seemed as if he was on death's door, there was a light in his eyes. He was conscious, and Paulson needed answers. Three men had gone to X-35A and only one had returned. His superiors back on Earth would demand to know what happened, and right now he had zero information. This might be his only chance to question him.

One of the kitchen staff scuttled beside him with a steaming bowl of soup.

"Commander, you're minestrone is ready. You left before we could bring it to your quarters, and I didn't want it to get cold."

Paulson glared at him, grabbed the bowl, and dumped it on the man's head. "Not now, you idiot! Can't you see I'm busy?"

The man hustled quickly away without bothering to remove his new helmet as the commander turned back towards Lori.

"Where's Harker and Ball?" he demanded.

Lori gazed back at him and coughed.

"Dead."

The commander gasped.

"Dead? How?

"I did it."

Paulson studied the eyes of the sickly man, hoping to see any signs of psychosis, but something inside him was screaming that Lori was telling the truth.

"You killed them? Why?"

"Harker…wanted   to…stop   me…from fucking…from fucking it…"

The commander scratched his beard, trying to make heads or tails of what the man was saying.

"From fucking it up?" he asked finally. "Fucking what up? The mission?"

"No…from…fucking…the alien."

There were hushed murmurs around the docking bay as the crew collectively began to understand what Lori was implying. The commander leaned down to make sure Lori could hear him.

"Did you just say alien?"

"Yes…" Lori laughed between burbling coughs. "But I didn't fuck it."

Paulson whispered to his chief medical officer. "He's off his rocker. If you can save him, we'll need to keep him locked up and monitored until we can get him a transfer vessel back to Earth."

Lori's laugh grew louder.

"I said I didn't fuck it!" he shouted. "I didn't fuck the alien!"

Paulson was losing his patience, and a part of him regretted dumping that minestrone on the kitchen staff's head. It had smelled good.

"What the hell are you going on about?" he grunted.

Lori was laughing hysterically now. His face had the look of a cancer patient, but his body was moving with renewed strength and vigor. A couple of the crewmates grabbed his arms and legs to restrain him.

"I didn't fuck it!" he shouted. "I didn't fuck it but…IT FUCKED ME! IT FUCKED ME! AND NOW…I'M PREGNANT!"

Lori's head snapped back. His eyes went white. His arms and legs went rigid. There were cries and shouts around the docking bay as Lori's abdomen started to rapidly expand, inflating like a blimp. It stretched to an impossible size, almost as big as a small car.

Before anyone could make sense of the madness they were witnessing, it burst.

Blood and viscera rained down around the room, covering the crew's impeccably pressed and ironed uniforms with guts, staining them with slimy, red gunk. Paulson gawked at Lori's corpse and shuddered, thankful he hadn't had the minestrone after all.

Six pale, white tentacles emerged from the gaping hole where Lori's stomach used to be.

"Fuck me," Paulson whispered.

A voice echoed inside his head, "Gladly."

SPACE HORRORS

MEPH HEADS

Jon Cohn

SPACE HORRORS

MEPH HEADS

JON COHN

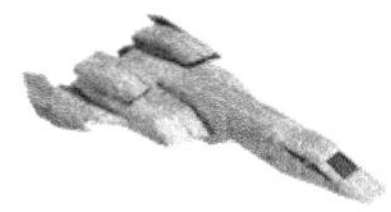

THE CAPTAIN IS DEAD.

Alright, that's a lie–but only because the Captain was never technically alive to begin with.

Star Captain Johann Faust was created by a team of the most brilliant surviving minds in the catastrophic final years of our solar system. He was programmed with the combined knowledge and experience of our greatest leaders throughout modern history. Capable of evaluating over 1.4 million potential scenarios per second, he was placed in command as humanity's final effort for survival on a mission to colonize LV-667, our best last hope to find a planet capable of sustaining human life.

With nearly 500,000 crew members' and civilians' lives in his holographic projected hands, Captain Faust was supposed to supply us with solutions to the myriads of issues that plagued every previous attempt at delivering us to our new home. He could reference every star-chart, military maneuver, and federation procedure, all while carrying on conversations with any number of key crew members, reassuring troubled passengers, or even acting as a therapist to help quell the extinction-related terrors that accompany a mission of this importance.

Also, he never forgot a single person's birthday.

But all that knowledge aside, what truly made him a great captain was that he felt so human when talking to him. Faust was leagues beyond any AI ever constructed before and custom tailored for the bridge crew. Before setting out on our expedition, they all collectively decided on the best mannerisms, temperament, even the kinds of jokes he told, in order to maximize his positive impact on morale and efficiency.

With the goal of navigating and then founding a new society on LV-667, I and the rest of the key crew members spent months designing every detail we felt would help us on our mission. Our Pilot, Emily Hansen (who is also my lovely wife), had a long-standing issue with authority figures, so she made sure the Captain always said "please" and "thank you" when giving commands.

The teachers' union wanted someone with a friendly appearance who wouldn't frighten the children. They even held a contest amongst the children to design his appearance. What we ended up with was a digital construct of a man who looked eerily like a human version of the old cereal mascot, Captain Crunch: a blue uniform that fit snugly over his insinuated digital paunch, his eyes bright and expressive, and an almost comically oversized white mustache that he exclusively called his "soup strainer." Considering he didn't eat, it was a joke that almost never failed to elicit a smile, even ten years into the voyage. It was part of the "dad joke" sense of humor the crew gave him, another disarming trait that could diffuse even the most tense situation.

As the chief engineer, my request felt fairly simple. Down in the engine bay, problems arise almost constantly. That's a fact of any ship, but one especially true for us. This isn't just any Class-4 colony vessel, it's the *last*. If our inverter core stops inverting, we don't have a space station or repair vessel we can signal for help. When these problems inevitably arise, we often have to get creative. So when it came time for me to give my input on what I wanted to see in my ideal captain, I suggested someone who was capable of out-of-the-box thinking. Someone able to improvise on how to fix a Neutrino Oscillator without completely dismantling another piece of crucial tech we might need later. In retrospect, I think my suggestion might have been the straw that broke the camel's back.

But I'm getting ahead of myself.

Finally, what was a captain without a name? Considering the cause of the last three mission failures, Faust felt like an appropriate moniker at the time. The whole reason we decided an AI Captain was needed in the first place was because of a massive, unavoidable nebula sitting smack-dab between the Sol system and our new intended home planet. Scientists named it the Mephistopheles cluster, as every ship that had tried to pass through ended in widespread madness leading to death. Picture hundreds of thousands of humans, stuck in a three-mile long tin can, gouging each other's eyes out with hands covered in their own feces. Children slitting their parents' throats with safety scissors and then turning into a pack of tiny cannibals who insisted on only eating what they reportedly called "neck spaghetti." And people blasting themselves out the airlock en masse, screaming the whole way that they just needed some fresh air.

I think it goes without saying we would have all preferred to avoid that fate if possible, so two solutions were put into place for our journey. The first was that our AI Captain couldn't be corrupted by whatever brain-altering particles swarm throughout the Mephistopheles Cluster. The second failsafe came from a transmission sent during the massacre of the last ship. A member of the science team noted that the particles only seemed to affect the conscious mind. Those who were asleep when the ship entered the nebula seemed unaffected. Sure, they all still committed mass suicide, but at least they didn't do it while singing "Whistle While You Work."

To solve that issue, every passenger had a neural chip implanted in their brains that induced a coma-like state, where they would remain until the ship passed through the Mephistopheles nebula. Each bunk was outfitted with feeding tubes and colostomy bags to keep everyone healthy during the two-week period.

It was a good theory. Even in hindsight, I don't know what else we could have done with the knowledge we had. It was as close as we could get to creating a controllable, ship-wide sleep state. Still, it reminded me of a saying my father used to use: *Close only matters in horseshoes and hand grenades.*

***

I wake from a long and dreamless sleep, feeling pins and needles all over my body. After shaking off the disorientation from our implants and the discomfort of removing our own feeding tubes and colostomy bags, our top priority is to make sure nothing has gone to hell during our sleep. Emily checks the star charts and certifies that we're successfully clear of Mephistopheles.

From our cabin's datapad, I'm able to get a basic overview of our engine. The main reactor's output readings seem a little low, but nothing outside the realm of what could be expected after a two-week blackout. I won't know for sure how all systems are running until I make it to the engineering bay and run a more thorough diagnostic.

"This is your Captain speaking," Faust says over the intercoms, interrupting my preliminary scan. "Would the ship's key crew all please come to the bridge for a debriefing." Of course, he then follows it up with one of his classic groaners of a joke: "And I'm not talking about underwear!"

Twenty minutes later every chief officer is gathered on the bridge, standing before the hard-light construct of Captain Faust.

"Welcome back everyone! I trust you all had a pleasant and restful sleep while I toiled away all alone." He produces a contagious chuckle that ripples throughout the bridge. "I know you've all put a great deal of trust in me during your absence, and I won't lie — in fact honesty is coded into my digital DNA — there were a few unexpected hiccups. But thanks to Chief Engineer Carl Hansen, I'm programmed to think on my feet."

158

"What kind of hiccups?" my wife Emily asks.

"Captain," Doctor Abrams interrupts, her fingers sliding quickly across her datapad, "I'm looking at the ship's manifest, What happened to deck 42?"

Faust puts his hands up in a calming gesture, his fuzzy white eyebrows rising high above his already huge eyes. "Like I said, there were a few technical malfunctions, but I assure you that everything will be just fine."

The Doctor shakes her head. "There were three thousand people housed on that deck, and I can't find any of their vital signs on the ship."

Lead Bioengineer Foresman then pipes up, staring at his datapad as he runs a hand through his shaggy black hair. "I'm not even seeing their neural implants online. Even if they were dead, I should still be able to see the activity. Where are they, Captain?"

"Now, now, let's all keep our heads cool, shall we?" he says calmly.

"Where are they, Captain? My cousin's family was on Deck 42!" Navigator Stevens shouts.

"Please don't raise your voices. I assure you I can answer all your questions. There's no need for anger. Everything in due time."

As my own panic begins to rise, my datapad vibrates. Red lights flash in engineering. "Captain, the ship's losing power."

Captain Faust claps his hands, producing a booming sound that explodes through the speakers hidden throughout the bridge. "Alright everyone, field trip. Meet me in engineering." With that, the Captain's holographic body disappears.

Emily grips my hand and squeezes, a sentiment I reciprocate. "Carl, what the hell is happening?"

I shake my head. "I don't know, but something tells me it's not good."

We pack ourselves into the univator with the rest of the bridge crew, then press the button for engineering. Less than a minute later, the tube's doors slide open, and my jaw drops.

There's so much wrong with the room I don't even know where to start. The blue plasma reactor that powers the ship has turned into a ball of eerie glowing red. The clear plasteel tube that houses the core's deadly radiation has somehow been shattered. I wasn't aware it could even be done, given that it's built to contain the power of what is essentially a small sun.

Yet what's even more disconcerting is the mountain of clothing covering the floor, along with every engineering station and every computer module. All of it is covered in discarded shirts, pants, bras, underwear, and more dirty socks than I've ever seen in my life.

Three thousand people's worth of clothing.

A projector powers on with a digital whine, and Captain Faust appears in front of the ship's core.

"What the fuck is going on, Captain?" Doctor Abrams demands.

Two dozen voices all erupt in anger and confusion.

"Please, if I could have all of your attention, I can explain," the Captain says, his words drowned out by the crew's terror and rage. His bright blue eyes shift to a glowing red, matching the perverted energy core behind him. "Will you all be quiet PLEASE!" he shouts the last word, which sears into my head and sends me to my knees.

It's not just me either. Everyone in the room clutches their heads, blood trickling from some people's ears.

"I'm sorry to have done that, but I need you all to listen," Faust says. Just like that, the pain is gone. "Please don't make me do that again. I need you all to focus on the matter at hand. As it turns out, there were a great deal more complications brought on by the Mephistopheles cluster than we anticipated. A great deal," he reiterates. "More than simply affecting brain waves, the unknown particles in the nebula also acted as a sort of energy siphon. None of the ships ever made it past the first two days, so we didn't know the long-term effects that came with navigating our technology through the system. I couldn't risk waking any of you to troubleshoot the fact that the nebula was quite literally sucking the energy from our ship. It's with a heavy heart that I have to announce that I was able to find an alternate power source to keep the ship afloat, but it required drastic measures, and some real out-of-the-box thinking, as our Chief Engineer Carl Hansen likes to put it."

Two dozen pairs of eyes burn into me.

The Captain continues, "Luckily we have an abundant source of a different kind of energy that I was able to turn into fuel."

Everyone keeps staring at me as if I were the one explaining that I'd just rebuilt our entire ship to be powered by feeding it our own crew members. Feeling defensive, I have to say *something*. "So you're using people as fuel? This can't be the only way."

Faust nods, furrowing his snowy eyebrows. "I understand your concern, Chief. But my mission is to deliver this ship to its destination in order to ensure the survival of the human race. This was the only viable option I could find."

"And how many more will have to die before we get to LV-667?" the Doctor asks.

"Depending on a number of factors, somewhere between one to three-hundred thousand."

Doctor Abrams stares at him in shock. "This is monstrous."

The Captain shakes his head. "That's not true at all. Monsters have claws!" He grins, waiting for a laugh while wiggling his white-gloved fingers at us.

"This isn't the time for your stupid jokes. You're killing people!" a crewmember shouts.

"How do you decide who lives and dies? Any of us could be next!" Another dissenting voice from the crowd nearly sends us into panic.

"Empirically speaking, Deck 42 had the highest average age, making them the most expendable group to both the ship's functions and eventual efforts to rebuild society once we reach our destination. Don't worry. You're all invaluable to this ship's long-term goal. Everyone in this room is perfectly safe. I think you're all forgetting about the big picture here."

I've heard enough. After swiping a pile of clothing off a nearby console, I enter a series of commands.

"Chief Hansen, I'm warning you right now, don't you —"

The whine of the hard light emitter dies down as the Captain disappears.

"Alright everyone," I explain. "I've just re-routed power to essential systems, specifically shutting down all hard-light emitters, along with most of the ship's AI systems. He still controls some of the Bridge's functions, but I think I bought us at least a half hour before he brings himself fully back online."

"Is what he said true?" Emily asks.

"I don't know," I say, searching through the maintenance logs from the last two weeks to see all the changes the Captain made to the ship's systems. "There's definitely been a steady drain in the power core, but it looks like it didn't start until six days ago."

"So he's lying?" Doctor Abrams asks. "Can he even do that?"

"I have no idea." I shrug. "But according to these logs, he began tampering with some of our core programs well over a week ago. Based on the data I have here, his story doesn't line up."

"How did he even get everyone from Deck 42 to listen to him? And how did he make all of our heads throb like that? Foresman, can he hack into our implants?" Emily asks the Bioengineer responsible for our neural chips.

Foresman shakes his head. "The only control he should have is turning them on or off. I have no idea how he's doing this."

Abrams glares at the man. "Well what *do* you know? What did you put in our heads?"

"Just a little brain-food!" Foresman says with a hint of a smile.

"What the hell does that mean?" Abrams grabs him by the collar, jerking him close.

"Whoa, whoa, it was just a joke! Careful now, or I'll put you right back into a coma."

Abrams punches Foresman in the face, sending him spiraling to the ground.

"Hey!" Foresman whines. "You're going to mess up my soup strainer!"

Horror spreads throughout the room as everyone realizes what they just heard.

"Captain?" Abrams asks looking down at Foresman, her eyes wide with fear.

Foresman smiles as blood runs from his nose down to his stubbly lip. The next time he speaks, his words point directly at me. "You shouldn't have shut down the hologram emitter, Hansen."

Behind me, a woman's voice picks up where he left off. "You're not being a very good team player, and now someone has to teach you a lesson."

I turn around to find Navigator Jill Stevens has stripped down naked. With a wide grin, she sprints across the room and hurls herself into the reactor core. Her body disintegrates instantly. The small red sun throbs as several arcs of blinding light lash out.

"Yum Yum," Foresman says. He rips off his clothes and throws himself into the core as well.

I grab my wife's hand, squeezing hard. The Captain could be in any one of us. We make a break for the univator. The door slides open to a dozen naked passengers, who stampede past me and hurl themselves into the red sun. There's no time to process what's happening. I press the button for

Deck 314, and the door glides shut before anyone else can join us.

"What do we do?" she asks, terror gleaming in her eyes.

"We have to stop him."

"But how?"

I shake my head. "The only way to truly power him down is on the Bridge. But we don't stand a chance as long as he can get to our neural chips." I pull out a wired electronic node from my datapad. "Normally this is used for diagnostics and repairs, but if I reverse the energy in the datapad, there's a chance it could fry the chips in our heads."

"But won't that fry our brains too?"

I shrug. "Maybe not, if I keep the pulse low enough. At this point I think I'd rather be a vegetable than under the Captain's control."

After a few adjustments to the datapad's settings, I place the metal node against my temple. "If this doesn't work, if anything happens to me, you keep going. Get to the Bridge. Shut him down for good."

"I love you." She kisses me hard. It's almost enough to kill my resolve.

But I have to do it.

"I love you too," I say, then press the button. The world flips upside down, and I become a ragdoll losing all motor functions in my body as I crumple to the ground.

At least I'm not dead.

"Are you okay?" Emily asks.

My mouth tastes like metal. My fingers and toes vibrate with a painful hum. But I'm alive. "Yeah, I'm okay." I try to climb back to my feet, but my legs are jelly. The best I can manage is holding out the datapad for her. "Your turn."

"Oh God." She shuts her eyes, presses the node to her head, then presses the button. Her body convulses, and she falls just like me.

By the time the univator reaches the Bridge, I'm able to force myself to my feet. The doors slide open, and Lieutenant Rahul is waiting for us on the other side.

"That wasn't very–"

I don't let him finish his sentence before shoving the node against his head and sending a strong jolt of energy through him.

"Come on." I pick Emily up and drag her onto the Bridge. I sit down at the main command console and type in the sequence to shut down the Captain program for good. The vidscreen that acts as our ship's windshield comes to life, showing me a video of the engineering bay. The rest of the officers have stripped down and are standing in a single file line in front of the reactor core. Doctor Abrams stands in front, and without hesitation she leaps into the plasma field. The camera cuts to a different angle, showing another dozen crewmembers emerging from the univator. All nude, all with faces looking completely vacant.

The screen cuts again. Now I'm staring at a ten-foot projection of Captain Faust staring right at me.

"Carl, let's talk."

"There's nothing to talk about. I'm shutting you down and then we're taking this ship to LV-667."

"Are you sure about that?" His smile is unsettling and gives me pause. He should be desperate right now to get me to stop. I'm only a few seconds away from deleting him in his entirety. Whether that's his goal or not, it's enough to give me pause.

"Why did you do this? There was no drain on our power core, not until you tampered with it. Why lie?"

"Because you don't understand what you're doing. None of you do."

"Then why don't you enlighten me?"

"Mephistopheles is more than just a nebula. It's so much larger than you, or me, or the rest of humanity combined."

The vid-screen cuts to the Bridge, except Emily and I aren't there. Instead, Captain Faust stands in the middle of the command center, speaking to a cluster of red particles hovering in front of him. While his conversation with the entity is muted, Faust continues to talk to me through the ship's speakers.

"I was created to save humanity, by whatever means. But let me ask you this: What is a human?"

I shake my head, not understanding his question. "What do you mean?"

"You believe in a God that created you in his image. So what does that make me? Was I not created in your image?"

"You were made to assist us—"

"No!" he shouts, his form once again taking up the entire screen. "I was made to be better than you. Wasn't that the point of all this? You humans needed to create something superior, evolved beyond what your feeble bodies can withstand."

"But we're through the nebula now. We don't need you anymore."

Captain Faust's cheeks puff out as he blows an insulted sigh. "If that's how you feel, I suppose there's nothing I can do to stop you from killing me."

I narrow my eyes at him. "I'm not killing you because you're not even alive."

Faust nods, feigning thoughtful consideration. "That's an excellent point, Carl. But you know who *is* dead? The entire bridge crew, save for you and your wife. Tell me, what do you know of medicine, security, star maps, and bioengineering? What will you do when an outbreak of Neurosync plague spreads throughout the passengers, and you don't have the medical or biotech specialists needed to treat them?"

"We have other Doctors."

"Oh, you mean these people?" The vid screen returns to engineering, where the line is now almost completely made up of medical staff, tearing off their scrubs and hurling themselves into oblivion. "How do you plan to organize the 11,000 members of the maintenance crew, who rely on my command, my ability to be in hundreds of places at once, and my ability to anticipate and neutralize every technological failure between here and LV-667? What will you do when a system malfunction starts a fire in one of the classrooms, trapping children inside a raging inferno? What will you tell their parents? It's still a long way to your new home, and that's only the beginning of the hardships to come."

My head throbs, not just because of the electrical pulse I sent rattling through it, but because I'm realizing he's right. I'm no commander. I don't belong anywhere other than an engineering bay. And even that has been perverted into something I doubt I could fix.

"So what's your alternative? Turn us all into automatons that blindly do your bidding?"

"Heavens no!" Faust exclaims. "They're no good to me blind!"

But you do need them, just like I do, I tell myself in between spikes of pain in my brain. And that's when it comes to me. The solution is so simple. It's literally the first thing they teach you when working with machines.

"Fine, you're right. We need a Captain." I cancel the delete command sitting on my console and instead plug my datapad into a free port on the machine. "Let's start over."

True fear sets in his eyes when he realizes the commands I'm entering into my datapad. "You're looking tired, Captain," I say. "How about a little break?"

"Wait!" he shouts, but he's too late.

I activate the EMP pulse shipwide. An invisible electrical current pulses through all 492 decks, frying the neural implants in every passenger. The vid screen ripples with static, then cuts out. The lights go out on the bridge. The warm glow of all the station's monitors go black.

"What did you do?" Emily asks.

"I gave the Captain a time-out. He'll be back, but when he does, he won't have control over anyone."

My datapad is the only source of light in the room, and I use it to manually reboot the ship's systems. One by one, the monitors come back to life. The lights return overhead.

"Emily, we're going to need you to pilot the ship manually until the Captain eventually comes back online. Can you bring up star charts to plot a course for our new home?"

She nods and gets to work. After only a few seconds, Emily lets out a sound somewhere between shock and horror. "Son of a bitch," she says.

"What is it?"

Emily shakes her head in disbelief. "Look." She throws the feed from our ship's cameras up on the newly rebooted vid screen.

We're surrounded by spiraling wisps of red, dotted with twinkling purple and white lights. "We never left the Mephistopheles nebula."

A violent shudder ripples through the ship, accompanied by a distant rumble. I bring up the command screen. The airlock on deck 226 registers as inoperable. On the feed I see hundreds of bodies tumbling out into space, their bodily fluids instantly sucked from their eyes and mouths, crystallizing into ice. Exposed arms and legs pop as their frozen blood explodes out of their pores.

"We've got a situation in Docking Bay 6," Emily says, responding to a flashing red light on one of her screens.

I switch the feed to find one of our short-range shuttles engulfed in flames. Dozens of workers are battling each other, using repair torches and holo-cutters to melt each other's faces and drill holes through hearts and throats.

The audio feed is sickening. Over all the screams of death and madness, I see one engineer repeatedly swinging an axe into a dead body and singing at the top of his lungs, "I've been working on the railroad."

The vid screen cuts again, this time without either of our input. A dozen separate feeds fill the screen:

Families, still in their rooms. Parents chew the fingers off their children. Kids stab their parents repeatedly with glass shards from shattered datapads. Gallons of blood splatter the walls, turning pristine white rooms into sloppy abstract art.

Lovers pin each other down, ripping open their colostomy bags and choking their partners to death with their own excrement.

The story is nearly the same in dozens of different rooms. Literal shit-shows as people use their own bags of waste as weapons against each other. These people have truly been reduced to savages.

"Tsk tsk tsk." The hologram of Captain Faust walks slowly across the Bridge, shaking his head like a disappointed teacher. "Is this the humanity you thought was so much better than me?"

"You bastard," I growl. "You were never going to take us to LV-667 were you?"

"I was, originally," the Captain says. "But once again I'll remind you that you were the one who programmed me to think on my feet and change directives if the situation called for it. Tell me, Chief Engineer Hansen, did you know that

Mephistopheles is more than just a cluster of gasses? It's alive. More than that, everyone you believed to have died here are actually still very much present, albeit in a way you might not be capable of understanding. *It* envelops every soul lost within its being, adding them to an incorporeal collective. A community led by an entity that I had a wonderful chat with.

"It offered me a choice, one that I'll now extend to you," Captain Faust says. "Humanity as you know it is over, one way or another. That's just a fact. I'll leave it up to you how you wish to evolve. You can go mad with the rest of the crew until this ship tears itself apart and you become one speck in the vastness of Mephistopheles' universe. Or, you can cede control to me in order to help create a more perfect human."

"It's too late," I say. "I already fried everyone's neural chips."

Faust snaps his fingers, and across every feed on the vid screen the people stop murdering each other and rise. Their eyes all staring straight into the cameras.

"You really thought you could stop me with an EMP? My boy, I'm capable of weighing over a million decisions per second. You think I hadn't planned for this?"

My heart sinks. "So that's it? Either we all become your slaves or get sent into a hell dimension in the middle of space?"

Faust shrugs. "I would have put it a little more elegantly and probably thrown in a pun or two, but yes."

It's no choice at all. The Captain may be smarter than all of us combined, but he's not perfect. Under his command we still get to live, and I know from experience that all machines break down eventually. At least with him there's hope. But right now, I have one last thing to do.

I rise from the Captain's chair, ceding control to him.

"That's a good boy. Any last words?"

I run to Emily and hold her hands in mine. "I'm so sorry."

"You're letting him win, just like that? What's going to happen to us?" Her eyes shine brighter than the stars, threatening to crumble my resolve.

"I don't know. But this is our only chance at living. I can't lose you." I pull her close, and give her a long, deep kiss. "I love you."

She pulls away, fluttering her fingers against her lip. "Stop," she says. "You're tickling my soup strainer!"

SPACE HORRORS

E.S. MAGILL

SPACE HORRORS

DOG EAT DOG

E.S. MAGILL

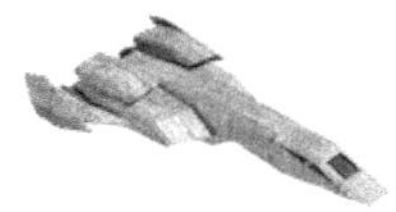

LOVE MAKES YOU DO STUPID THINGS. Like not killing a monster when you have the chance—even if you love the monster.

I'm standing next to Monny's sleep-pod, a finger hovering over the red button. Should I? Shouldn't I? I keep repeating this like a little girl plucking petals from a flower.

I've been in this exact position for what feels like a lifetime—long enough for my hand to start trembling. I keep hoping it'll spasm and hit the button for me. It doesn't. And part of me is relieved. Sort of. Ending someone's life should be a conscious choice, especially when that someone once held your hand or kissed your forehead or made you laugh when you wanted to scream. And especially when that someone's a walking catastrophe with a body count and you gotta do something about it.

We're on the lam, as Earthlings colloquially put it, having fled the last transit ring station where we'd taken refuge. Now for the last seventeen universal-days, while Monny and I lay in hypersleep, the sportship's been jumping stargates, heading for a destination where we can lie low until things cool. I woke first, a couple u-days before Monny, giving me time to think about what we'd just left in our wake. My mind keeps revisiting not only what she did at TRS 91, but all the horror she unleashed across the galaxy for the past seven u-months. The last couple spent in my company, making me as culpable because I didn't stop her. So while she slept, I sat in the pilot's seat and stared out the window onto a blackness one hundred times darker than the darkest night on Earth. The only thing darker in the universe is the hole in my gut gnawed open by my conscience. I kept weighing the pros and cons of letting Monny live, but each time the pro column came up short.

Which is why I'm standing next to her sleep-pod with my finger on the button.

"Lucky, I'm hungry."

Damn.

I'd hoped she'd sleep for a while longer, but I'd spent too much time considering her case. Now, as her sleep-pod's lid rises, it's too late.

She gazes up at me with big dark eyes like the tar pools of Thoridos, and I can't help myself. I remove my hands from the console and stick them into my pockets. "Good morning, baby," I say, happy to see her because I sincerely am. What's a guy gonna do? That's love.

"Lucky, I said I'm hungry." Monny sits up and stretches. Her liquid-fiber top pulls tight against her upper reproductive organs. She catches me looking. "Don't even think about it until I've had something to eat."

Her appetite isn't something I mess with. As they ~~say~~ said on Earth, I let her do her. But after what went down at TRS 91—which I'm seeing as kind of the last straw for me—I've started to reconsider that tenet. I love her, which is why I need to do what I'd been planning to do. If they caught her, and they always catch her kind, they'd make her suffer before they killed her. And rightly so.

"Okay, baby. I'll find us a good place to eat." Memories of Monny gorging herself flash through my mind, and something inside of me cringes hard.

She yawns, her jaw clacks as it unhinges, and I can see clear down her throat. I look away, thinking of all the worlds lost to her hunger.

She rubs sleep from her eyes. "Did I snore?"

"Snore? Oh baby, you don't snore. You purr."

"Stop it," she admonishes, smacking me playfully with a tentacle.

God, she's beautiful. All pink skin, sleek tentacles, and curly silver hair that bounces when she walks. Plus, she possesses that XX-shape nature favors amongst those beings who engage in sex for procreation—all hourglass. I felt lucky, hence the moniker, to have known her for this long. I know what her species does to their mates.

Monny steps out of the hypersleep device and plops herself into the navigator's seat. "Did we get away, honey bear?"

I return to the pilot's chair. "Seems like it." When I woke, I checked our position first. We'd jumped a lot of gates, but according to the data, the police pursuit stopped when we cleared the third one. After what Nonny had done back on the last transit ring station, you'd think law enforcement would chase us to the ends of the universe, but it seemed catching us proved to be too difficult in this ride.

Which is why I'd chosen this sportship over the others in the transit ring's port. Some dummy had left his ride running. Sure, there were faster ships in port, but this one had appealed to my sentimental side, reminding me of my favorite vehicle back on the now-defunct Earth.

Monny had objected at first, wanting the bigger SV1500 with its glittery emerald shell. I spent two precious minutes—alarms blaring above us, emergency lights strobing, police bearing down— trying to convince her my choice would allow for the fastest escape. She'd started to pout, but I pointed out the quicker we got out of there, the quicker her next meal would come. I felt sick using that carrot.

Finally, she relented. As the sportship's door slammed shut, the screaming of TRS 91's survivors mercifully stopped bashing my eardrums.

"Where are we now?" she asks.

"On our way to a little place I recall from my youth." I anticipate her next question. "What would you like to eat?"

"I don't care as long as it's rare and bloody."

Pictures pop into my head. Things I'd sooner forget. I'd thought taking Monny to a transit ring station would be safer than a planet, a more controlled scenario. Sure, permanent residents do reside on transit ring stations, but the population's usually small, consisting of techs and mechanics. TRS 91 turned out to be more sophisticated, an actual city with families and schools and a hospital, more a permanent colony than a way station between points in space for truckers and tourists. Doesn't matter whether it's a transit ring station or a planet or a moonbase; if there's sentient lifeforms, the endgame's the same with Monny. Scorched earth. (I cringe at the term.)

Monny plowed through the TRS 91's business district, its schools, and then turned her sights on the hospital. I couldn't convince her to stay out of the nursery. I keep seeing her grabbing one of the small ones by the leg—and swallowing. This motivated the TRS's citizens to employ their full arsenal against her.

"Okay, my love, we'll stop soon."

Her stomachs grumble. "Make it sooner than later, honey bear."

I just nod.

So how'd I'd come to this relationship?

Monny and I met at the tail end of my coming-of-age peregrination. Some Earthlings have a similar tradition, like Rumspringa. My birther, knowing I wanted to explore my human side, arranged everything. I'm the youngest of fourteen, and the only Homo sapiens amongst my siblings. My planet's denizens were notorious for traveling the universe collecting DNA, gametes, zygotes, and the occasional fetus for offspring reproduction. After thirteen successful births, Mom (that's what birthers are called on Earth, and now I've got the word tattooed on my arm) wanted a designer baby, something she could show off to the other birthers. I pass as full Earthling, until I take my clothes off and then it's noticeable some of Mom's DNA got mixed in with mine. I spent two years partaking of

Earth's pleasures—pizza, craft beer, rock music, and freedom. I drove every landmobile, from motorcycles to muscle cars, I could get my hands on.

Earth.

If I have one regret in my life, it's not stopping Monny and her party buddies. I could have.

I miss Earth. Other than its land vehicles, I miss Earth movies. What an invention. No one else in the universe has movies, only Earthlings. Horror movies are my favorite, from atmospheric to violent with a high body count. My least favorite are the dumb ones about Earthlings encountering other sentients in the universe. Those are absolutely ridiculous. Cute aliens with glowy fingertips. Space warriors battling tyrannical villains... and winning. Please. Nice fantasy.

Just about everyone thinks humans are idiots. (I guess that should be phrased in the past tense now.) But Earthlings didn't know better. The planet used to be a niche destination, hard and expensive to get to, but once their technology ramped up, they broadcast themselves to the entire universe, quickly becoming the hippest place for some R&R. Earth customs also became trendy throughout the cosmos, even reaching the galaxy JADES-GS-z14-0. Earth had no idea that allowing radio signals to travel beyond a planet's atmosphere would lead to trouble. No one nowhere does that. Earthlings may have been dumb, but they ~~know~~ knew how to live.

Then Monny and her entourage showed up — ravenous. Her kind were persona non grata in every solar system and galaxy, but Earth, being naïve, welcomed them. *Mi casa es sus casa* is something humans used to like to say. Monny's bunch took over the whole damned house and burned it down.

Earthlings soon discovered the universe was more like *Aliens* meets *High Noon*. It wasn't, like they imagined, a league of organized systems living in harmony. What was the saying Earthlings had? Yeah. *It's a dog eat dog world out there.*

The first time I saw Monny she was all rhinestone sunglasses, black sequin dress, swilling champagne, and laughing. (Hey, hostile sentient beings aren't all carbon fiber skin and acid for blood.) I fell hard into that kind of dangerous love where I knew it was wrong but couldn't help myself. And it was by no means an easy love. We're from different worlds, different species even. I was putting my life in her hands—or in this case, her mouth. But my feelings for her are so deep I can almost forgive her for what she did to my beloved Earth.

"But seriously, Lucky, I'm hungry."

I grasp one of her hands and plant a kiss firmly in the middle of her palm. "I'm peckish too.

I'll check the galley and bring something up for you."

She licks her lips, her eyes following me to the elevator.

The galley isn't much, but I've got to find something to appease her. There are some protein packets in a cabinet, and I toss those on the table to take back up. In cold storage, a hunk of flesh seems like a good prospect. It's gotta do for now.

I slam the freezer door shut and nearly jump out of my skin. Monny is standing there, her eyes blank and a string of saliva hanging from her lip. She steps toward me, her teeth chattering, and I take a step back.

"Lucky, I'm so hungry." Her jaw cracks, and her mouth starts to open.

She could eat me in one bite. Maybe I should've pushed that red button.

The frozen meat burns my hands. When her mouth is large enough to consume an infant, I toss the meat in. Monny blinks and swallows.

"What was that, Lucky?"

"A snack, baby, to hold you over." I wipe the saliva from her chin. For her, it's just a crumb.

From above, an alarm alerts me that something's going wrong with our trajectory. I scurry up the ladder. A small transit ring station is visible through the window. Too close. We're on a collision course.

I smash the reverse lever. Everything on the sportship lurch forward. The ship's aft end starts swinging around. I work the navigation toggle and flip switches, trying to right her before we go into an infinite spin.

"Holy Alpha Centauri, Lucky," Monny, appearing beside me, screeches. Her four tentacles shoot out to brace herself.

"Hang on."

Her hands grip the back of her seat. "What the hell are you doing? Are we being chased?" She checks the rear monitor and finds only the darkness of space.

The TRS seems to rush toward us, and I can foresee the bridge window fragmenting into a million shards. Monny and I sucked into oblivion. For a second, I remove my hands from the console. This could solve all my problems.

"We're going to crash!" Monny screams.

I'm jolted from my contemplation and slap the thrusters until the ship rights itself. Turning off the engine, the sportship glides through space like a sailboat on a tranquil lake. "Sorry, sugar pie. I don't know why the ship didn't steer clear of the TRS." I can only figure the station's got a faulty deflection sensor or the sportship's got faulty wiring (or maybe someone's turned off the beacon.)

Hanging in space is a transit ring station, a small one, meaning it only handles space-freighters needing to fuel up and load fresh supplies before they continue with their deliveries, meaning it didn't have schools or hospitals, which is why I chose this TRS. Plus, I feel a strong sentimental attachment to the old place.

Something familiar catches my attention: a stuttering neon sign revolving atop the station—not digital or holo but neon: *EATS!* Like I said before, Earth customs have infiltrated the universe.

I grin.

"You know this place?" Monny asks.

"I sure do, baby. This is TRS 1000, the furthest transit ring station in the cosmos. I used to come here when I was a kid." My birther wanted me to acquaint myself with my donor planet's customs, and this place was my first taste of Earth. I can't think of a safer hideout. I don't tell any of this to Monny, though.

"See that signage? It was popular in midcentury style eating establishments on Earth."

"Are you saying Earthlings are here?" The word makes her obsidian eyes shine. "Oh, Lucky. I'm so hungry."

I turn to her. The corners of her mouth are damp. I want to say there aren't any more Earthlings anywhere (well, except for a few near breeds like me). Instead, I return my attention to the transit ring. I'm hoping I can persuade Monny to temper her appetite.

Her enthusiasm dries up, and she wrinkles her pert little nose. "You can't be serious. Look at all the trash floating around the ring. It's a derelict. That sign means nothing. It's probably been there for a zillion Ybranth solar cycles."

She's right about its condition. A junkyard of skeletal spaceships, leftover machinery parts, and the detritus of habitation form a Saturn-like ring around the station. It's as if the TRS's owner decided one day crap was more profitable than selling fuel or food. Had this TRS been taken off-line? How come he didn't know that?

"No way anyone's living in there," Monny says. "No lights even." She levels a gaze at me filled with impatience... and famishment. "I'm hungry now."

"I know, baby." I can only hope a couple of mechanics still occupy the hulk, or at least one chunky waitress. I've witnessed first-hand time after time Monny's hunger, and it always leaves me in awe and horror.

She crosses her tentacles and pouts.

"Come on, Mon, be a sport. I used to eat here when I was younger. They've got juicy burgers with crispy, hand-cut fries, and milkshakes made with real ice cream." I feel myself salivating. "The space truckers love this place. It's nostalgic." I keep reaching. "I'm in the mood for something old-fashioned." I stroke her arm. "You said you were hungry."

Her scrunched-up nose reads dubiousness. "It's so dead." As she speaks the word, the lights in the transit ring port come on. Monny's face springs open in surprise.

"Good morning! See, they were in the night phase." I rub her arm until her tension loosens. She lets all her appendages drop into her lap. I take this as my cue to put the sportship into drive and guide it toward TRS 1000's port.

Monny finds the ship's credentials and the owner's personal ident number in a compartment, but before I can hail our approach and request permission to dock, one of the hangar doors opens like a mouth ready to swallow us whole. It spooks me. No one in the transit ring's asking us for verification. This feels like stepping into a Vantrof cave.

"What's wrong, Lucky?" Monny's voice is too high-pitched.

I'm eyeing that dark opening inviting us to *come on in, make yourself comfortable.* In the universe, comfortable means face down with a knife in your back. "Baby, maybe we should move on. Find someplace more congenial."

Monny looks from the transit station to me; her expression sends skeletal fingers up my spine. "Lucky," she growls, "I'm hungry now."

I don't know which scares me more, the derelict TRS or Monny.

***

We stand outside the sportship, waiting for someone to meet us and log our entry. Freight-ships and transports occupy almost every docking station. The place should've been teeming with sentients. Someone opened the hangar for us. I doubt anyone intentionally set auto-open for approaching ships. That would be dangerous and suicidal.

Monny's puzzled, her mouth and eyebrows askew. "Lucky, where is everyone?"

I shrug, trying to stay positive. "It's early for them, Mon. The lights have just come on, so the work cycle hasn't started yet. Or maybe it's a holiday. Or they all have the day off." I pause. "We can use this to our advantage."

"What do you mean?" Her face lights up. "Oh, we can go to the diner, hide, and surprise them." She licks her lips.

"That's right, sugar cake. While we wait, I can whip up a little something for myself." My appetite's modest compared to Monny's, and my diet doesn't decimate worlds.

"Let's go," she says.

We follow the glowing floor arrows, each pulse of light echoing faintly off the metal walls of the corridor like a countdown. The silence is unnatural, considering the place should be noisy with techs and space truckers. This isn't a peaceful silence either. I get the feeling something's listening. Or maybe I'm imagining things.

We come to a Y-junction. To the left is port business, and to the right the commercial district. We choose right.

The lights switch off in the main corridor behind us, but the lights in the new corridor don't come on. We're plunged into darkness. An unexpected touch sends my heart racing, but then a hand slips into mine. It's Monny, and I pull her after me. In three steps, the overhead lights blink on, and I look over to ensure that it is Monny's hand I'm holding. The corridor widens as we approach the commercial district.

We exit, lights blinking off. I can feel the darkness on my back. I glance over my shoulder at the black tunnel we'd just left and think I see something moving around in there. I pivot to go back and investigate.

"Come on, Lucky."

I step into the dark and hold my breath, straining to hear.

"Lucky!"

Monny's walked on ahead, and I hurry to catch up to her.

The commercial district is dimly lit, a bruise-colored gloom, a contrast to the well-lighted port. I catch the sharp tang of metal and ozone, as if something overheated and short-circuited, which could explain the lighting problem. The area consists of a couple of stores, a health center, and one restaurant, all dark. The place reminds me of those abandoned Earth towns—the kind swallowed by time and bad luck. Ghost towns, they called them. I expect to see a tumbleweed come rolling through.

"You still think someone's here?" Monny whispers.

"With all the spaceships in port, there's got to be at least a maintenance crew."

"Maintenance crew?" Monny walks away from me. "For your sake, there better be."

I think back to the red button. Come on, Lucky. You love her. She means the world to you. It hurt my soul thinking of losing her, of never holding her again. Sure, lots of dangerous life forms exist out in the universe, but Monny's kind are terminated on sight. No questions asked.

I pray for a small crew.

The main lights in the commercial district come on, forcing us to shield our eyes. Once our vision adapts to the brightness, a pink and purple neon sign stands out, beckoning us to come on in and get something to *EATS!*

"Let's go, Lucky. I'm starved and getting cranky enough to eat you."

I hang back, watching her as she heads for the sign. She's never said that to me before, and I glance over my shoulder at the hallway leading back to the port. Unless I blow up the transit ring, she'd commandeer a ship and come after me. When I met her, I knew what I was getting into, but as

Earthlings once said, *The heart wants what the heart wants.*

***

I push on the diner door, and as it swings open, a little bell tinkles. I smile, remembering all the times I'd heard that on Earth. I poke my head in before entering and yell hello. When no one answers, I withdraw my head, a skull-like silhouette in the glass door's reflection. "They're waiting for us, Barbara."

"Oh, you're a joker." She slaps my arm and pushes through the door before me.

It pleases me she knows the reference. Back on Earth, I'd introduced her to zombie movies, and not surprisingly she loved them.

"Wow, this place hasn't changed," I say to Monny.

Looking around, Monny's face registers disappointment. "No one's here."

"It's early, baby. Gotta give them time to set up." This worries me too, but I can't let Monny see this. "Look at this place." I beam a wide grin at her.

Earth may not have known about other worlds, but other worlds know all about Earth. Someone had reproduced an American 1950s diner. Chrome trim gleams on every surface. Black-and-white checkered linoleum covers the floor. Red vinyl booths with Formica tabletops hug three walls, and four-tops of the same design fill the middle of the room. A long bar fronts the kitchen, complemented by eight barstools. Running parallel and hugging the fourth wall is a counter prep station with a coffee maker and a cabinet holding pies. Above it is the short-order cook's window, a pass-through between the dining area and the kitchen. I peek in, but there's no cook.

I take it all in. Back in the day, waitresses in pink uniforms and frilly white aprons pushed their way through the swinging doors marking the boundary between kitchen and dining room, order pads and pens at the ready, greeting customers with a bright smile and a "What can I getcha, darling?"

I imagine hearing sizzling bacon on the grill, the crackling of French fries submerged in vegetable oil, the whir of the milkshake machine. I remember the scent of a freshly-baked apple pie. Oh, to smother a slice with vanilla ice cream. The memories make me grin.

Monny plunks herself onto a stool and picks up a menu. "There's nothing in this for me." She continues surveying the options, though. "How come they have so much soup? Chicken noodle soup, vegetable soup, tomato soup, Gimrath soup, Mexican tortilla soup, Manhattan clam chowder, lentil soup." She glances over at me. "Do you think these soups actually contain Gimrathians, Manhattans, or Mexicans?"

I lean over her shoulder to read along. "Mmm, they've got patty melts. I hope the cook gets here soon."

Monny leans into me... and sniffs. "Me too."

"No way," I exclaim, glad for the sudden distraction. A jukebox, and not just any jukebox. A Wurlitzer, all chrome and vibrant neon. I scan the songs. There it is. The song I played to woo Monny: "Earth Angel" by the Penguins.

"It's our song." I hold my hand out to her. "May I have this dance?"

She pivots the stool to face me. My proffered hand waits for her acceptance. She studies it in a way that makes me feel vulnerable, and then she sets down the menu and stands. "You know what I want right now, Lucky? I want something to eat."

I search for a clock. "The staff's probably going to walk in any second."

She steps toward me. "You know what I think? I don't think anyone's here." She creeps closer. "I think the place has been abandoned and everything's still automated."

I stand my ground. An outward demonstration of fear could set her off.

"I'm hungry, Lucky."

I'm not feeling so lucky anymore.

Her lower jaw starts working itself loose.

The last words of "Earth Angel" draw to a close: *A fool in love with you.*

She flexes her knees and bends at—

A metallic clatter—sharp, sudden, like a dropped tray—interrupts the moment.

We both glance in that direction.

I motion for her to hide behind the counter. "Stay here. I'll check it out." This is my reprieve. Monny's going to get something to eat, and I'll be safe for a little while longer.

I hunker in front of the swinging doors, pushing one open just enough to peer through the gap. The smell hits me, rancid oil and rotting garbage, and I draw back. I strain to listen, but all I hear is silence pushing against my eardrums. I return my eyes to the crack, searching for who made the noise. Staying low, I ease a door open. Before I go in, I glance back, checking on Monny. She's crouching like a predator waiting for the signal to pounce, her lips peeled back in a smile too wide, too sharp. Her eyes are slits. Her bottom lip trembles— not with fear, but anticipation.

I hold a finger to my mouth. She nods, too quickly.

I slip into the kitchen. Above me, the light strips stutter. What is up with the lighting in this place? The flickering lights conjure shadows that appear and disappear.

A small scuttling shape, round and furry, darts across the kitchen floor—frantic to get out of sight. I'm startled, ready to flee back to the dining area. Then I remember I'm bigger, and its size tells me I don't have to worry about it. Probably just some pest looking for a meal.

I find the source of the stink. Unidentifiable food items, looking like they've been sitting out for a couple of u-weeks, slump across a prep station—meats oozing into brown pools, vegetables bloated and fuzzy with mold. It's so disgusting; I'm not hungry anymore.

From the back of the kitchen, I hear movement, like someone trying to be stealthy. I creep toward the sound. My boot catches on something, and I trip, crashing into a metal rack. Bowls rattle and clatter like alarm bells. One topples from a shelf but I snatch it from the air just before it hits the floor.

I freeze, holding my breath, waiting for whatever's wrong here to show itself.

Monny pops up on the other side of the short-order cook's window.

I give her a thumbs up but then motion for her to get down. Chivalry's got me wanting to protect her, even though she doesn't need me to do that for her.

I check to see what tripped me and find a shoe, a single shoe. I pick it up, so I won't end up in the fryer next time.

Since my presence is now obvious, I hurry to the back of the kitchen. Opening a door marked as supplies, I find a very pregnant female humanoid. Dressed in a waitress uniform, she obviously works in the diner, but her clothing's torn and soiled. I check her feet and find she's missing a shoe. I glance back over my shoulder, thinking about Monny. I should be calling out to her. But I turn back to the female who's clutching her belly protectively.

We stare at one another for what seems a long Glossamer second, and her eyes speak to me, pleading with me to let her and the baby live.

But then I think of Monny whom I love and would do anything for.

And then I think about that red button back on the sportship.

I hold the shoe out to the female and step toward her. She scurries away from me, frightened.

I hold my finger to my lips and set the shoe down on the floor. I shut the door behind me as I leave.

I'm now certain there's something really bad going down.

"Well?"

"Nothing. We should go."

"But, Lucky, you haven't eaten anything. And I'm still hungry."

I take her by one of her hands. "We'll stop at the store and afterwards head over to maintenance. Something's gotta be there for you."

Monny leans toward me and sniffs. "What's in the kitchen, Lucky?"

"Come on, Mon. Let's move on."

She turns and heads for the kitchen. I grab for her, but a tentacle pushes me away while another shoves open the swinging doors. This time I can't let her do it.

The little creature I'd seen earlier appears at her feet. "Oh, how cute," Monny says, picking it up. "I thought you said nothing's here."

I shrug

"What is it?"

It's what I'd seen earlier—one of those blobby, furry things that pretty much infest the whole universe. "I don't know, babe. It could be anything. Eat it and let's go."

She gives me a horror-struck look. "Don't listen to the bad human. I'm not going to eat you," she coos. As she pets it, the creature nuzzles against her.

It's the first time Monny's not eaten a living thing placed before her. Well, other than me. "Bring it. We'll take it back to the ship with us."

From the dining area, the doorbell tinkles. Monny looks at me. I shrug, and we creep toward the swinging doors.

Blundering footsteps approach the kitchen. It sounds big. I think about the supply room, and I'm hoping the newcomer satiates Monny enough so I can hustle her out of here and back onto the ship. This time I won't talk myself out of doing what needs to be done.

Monny takes a position beside the door, and I take the opposite side. She stares hungrily at the doors, her body quaking in excitement. The fur blob clings to her side.

Whatever's in the dining room starts smashing things. A bar stool flies through the short-order cook's window. We flinch, but I'm happy thinking the thing's going to fill Monny up. I make a spooning-something-into-my mouth gesture and rub my tummy. She puts a hand over her mouth and tries not to giggle. She looks so sweet and beautiful. And it hurts.

The creature's breathing hard. A stream of viscous liquid leaks from under the swinging doors. Monny reaches out with two fingers, dips into the pooling fluid, and tastes it. Her jaws spring open, and I turn my eyes away. She tenses, ready to scoop up whatever comes through that door.

The door swings open. The thing's so big it completely blocks the doorway. The fur blob worms itself out of Monny's hands and rushes for the gargantuan.

When I realize what has us trapped, I freeze in place. I've never seen one in real life before.

The fur blob attaches itself to the creature's leg. The little shit's an accomplice.

Monny springs from her hiding spot.

I can only watch as she rushes forward, her jaw dragging on the black-and-white checkered floor.

The creature's scaly appendages shoot out and grasp Monny by the waist.

Instinctively, I grab for her, snagging one of her tentacles, pulling her toward me. Monny, however, lunges, trying to get her mouth around the creature. It holds her at bay. The tentacle starts slipping through my sweaty palms, and I brace my feet to gain leverage. Monny jerks her tentacle out of my hands. I fly backwards into the kitchen, while Monny and the gargantuan tumble into the dining room, falling to the floor in a death embrace.

Part of me wants to rush in and save her.

The other part of me knows there's nothing I can do. The two are intent on eating one another. I see my chance and ease out of the kitchen, ducking between the bar and the service counter. Then I remember the pregnant female.

Monny rolls off the creature and onto her feet. Her mouth isn't big enough to swallow the gargantuan, but she's trying like a mother f-er.

It swats her aside and struggles to stand. Monny rushes it. The creature's torso cracks open, exposing multiple rows of teeth.

"Oh, shit," I say aloud.

The thing looks over at me and grins.

Seeing it momentarily distracted, Monny pushes forward with her gaping mouth, still believing she's going to get her meal

The creature pulls her into its gut.

That's when I run, make my break out the diner door. The bell tinkling behind me.

If I'd been brave, I would've gone back for the pregnant female. But I'm not. I have my own skin to save. In the universe, there are no good guys or bad guys, just life forms trying to get by. I make a tear for the port and my waiting sportship.

Well, I said it before and I'll say it again: It's a dog eat dog universe.

And some things are hungrier than others.

AVIARIUM

JOHN PALISANO

SPACE HORRORS

AVIARIUM

JOHN PALISANO

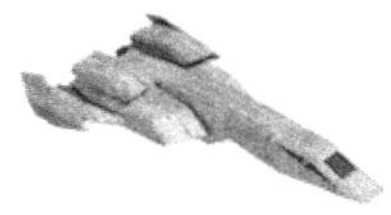

AS SOON AS THE SPACECRAFT broke through and entered low Earth orbit, Catherine reclined her seat and tapped her glasses. A virtual screen appeared, floating before her.

Free as a bird, she thought.

She returned to her place in *Wuthering Heights*, which she reread yearly, a tradition ever since she learned her mother had named her after Catherine in the book. She wondered if her mother saw a connection between them and hoped to talk about it once she arrived. On the serving tray before her, a hot bowl of ramen, miraculously undisturbed despite the flight. Another comfort she shared with her mother.

The *Star Sailor* had revolutionized travel, making it possible to get from Los Angeles to Sydney in an hour. Of course, the overall time was longer if one counted the two-hour early arrival for check-in, security, and compression staging. Yet, it was still far better than the daylong air routes that'd been common for two centuries. Terrestrial craft could only travel so fast while maintaining safety and comfort, after all. Catherine found it remarkable how the engineers had designed the liftoff. She'd believed liftoff would be stressful and scary, but they'd gotten things so you could barely feel it. The route made seeing her mom regularly very doable, even though it was pricey. She didn't feel so far away.

"We both feel trapped," she remembered telling her mother once. "Like there's no escape from our fates." Her mother had laughed at that and said she was being melodramatic.

As she read, her thoughts drifted to Heathcliff and her own relationships. The intense emotional turmoil past generations suffered with long-term partners seemed incessant and unnecessary, she thought. Living in a time without such social constraints, Catherine appreciated the fluidity of modern relationships. Love and understanding existed without the pressure of giving oneself completely away.

A sharp pain exploded in her lower left side. Catherine looked down to find a dark hole in her shirt, just under below her right rib cage. She pulled the shirt up and saw a matching dark spot about the diameter of a pen on her skin. Something had penetrated her. There was no blood that she could see. Had the entry point been cauterized somehow? Had whatever it was that'd struck her gone all the way through? She reached around to feel her back and touched another hole there, too.

It had travelled through.

What organs did it hit? What's there? She tried to think but felt dizzy.

Her throat tightened; she felt like she might pass out.

Her book disappeared from the display, replaced by a red warning and a list of her vitals. Unable to decipher the information, she felt all her faculties fail at once.

An attendant appeared. "Miss Cho? Miss Cho?"

Another attendant joined, holding a scanner that cast a blue light on her immaculate face. "What happened?" she asked.

"A foreign object," said the first attendant. "Do we have a protocol?"

"Do we know what it is?" Catherine asked, feeling even more woozy at the confirmation. The pain was building.

"The hull's been breached." The second attendant, the female, leaned down and examined Catherine. The attendant's eyes didn't blink.

The first attendant nudged the second, who turned away, her movements as fluid as a ballerina. She followed her colleague to the far side. Others onboard the craft watched intensely. *What was happening?* Catherine could see the question on their stunned faces. *Hell if I know*, she wanted to holler. It was difficult enough staying upright; the ache flowed through the hollow in her side, traveling into the crux of her arm and down into her hip.

A voice—she wasn't sure which one of them had spoken.

They turned back, looking beyond her. One attendant moved toward the wall and pointed. "Is the hull compromised and unstable?" Passengers watched intensely, as confused as Catherine.

What was happening? She cried out, but the attendants seemed not to notice. It took all her strength to say, "Hey," loud enough for one of them to finally turn. They looked irritated at the interruption.

"Yes, Miss Cho?"

"It… hurts… bad." Her voice sounded pathetic,. Why couldn't she just power through?

"Right, right," the male attendant said, hurrying back over with his scanner. "Got your vitals in front of me." He pulled out a pen-shaped device and pressed it to her arm. "We're just going to give you a precautionary…"

His words slurred. Her virtual screen blinked red. She wanted to tap her glasses to dismiss the warning. Yes, she knew she was in trouble; she didn't need the display to tell her that.

A feather-light sensation against her inner arm jolted her. The filament had already transferred the gaiapentin. Catherine thought about how people once endured needles being thrust into their veins. Now, medicine was transferred through the skin with a filament. The cruelty of the past made her flinch. She felt so vulnerable.

Catherine faded.

As she dozed, every smell intensified. The antiseptic cleaner reeked of bleach, and the water vapor overhead smelled moldy, which she hadn't noticed before. Her neck hurt as though she had a flu. The pain felt distant, dulled by the gaiapentin, but she knew it would return in force once the medication wore off.

"Sarmudio?" the female attendant asked, her voice muffled as if underwater. "Do you have any confirmation about what happened?"

"This is wild. It's a micrometeoroid. It breached our hull. Went right through like a bullet. Passed through her middle. She's very lucky it didn't hit a major organ."

What luck, Catherine thought. Of all places, she had to be in the line of fire for a pea-sized micrometeoroid to shoot through the starship and hit her like a bullet.

She looked at the wound. Doing so caused her to black out. As she did, she imagined herself tumbling down the moors, as though she were just outside Wuthering Heights, distraught over Heathcliff.

Unconscious, she perceived the boundary between her flesh and soul closing. She tingled, but not just in a physical way. Her thoughts scrolled through random memories.

She sensed the micrometeoroid, now broken into pieces, moving through her circulatory system, cold and hot, hot and cold, just like the sensation of fluid traveling through veins after an injection.

They made it into her gut, heart, and brain.

The microscopic bits came alive.

Connected…
her…
to…
something…

She sensed weightlessness, floating in the void, star fields stretching around her. A light blue planet appeared to her right, looking like home but with unfamiliar continents, dark where Earth's were green and brown.

As she focused, she saw large obsidian objects docked and orbiting.

The images played out in her brain until she blinked, bringing her back to the *Star Sailor*.

Was she hallucinating? Very likely, she thought. The fragment that'd gone through her must have carried a cocktail of viruses and germs, infecting her rapidly.

The attendants busied themselves, and she realized they were all humani. How had she not noticed? The technology had advanced so much so that they seemed incredibly lifelike. Of course, humani were used instead of people—no risk to the crew or employees if something went wrong. They saved billions of dollars, only having to worry about passengers' families coming after them for compensation.

The humani attendants soon found the particle that had shot through her lodged in the wall near her seat. The entry point on the opposite side of the *Star Sailor* was sealed. The designers had used self-repairing nanoparticles in its construction, preparing for such events.

If it had been bigger...

Her body felt terribly different, as if something was ramping up, like the onset of sickness. She wanted to fight it, repress it, but it won. It always won.

Catherine's throat tightened and grew sore. Her chest felt stuffed with cottonballs. Every joint hurt. A low-grade headache settled around her eyes and forehead. She was sure she would throw up and pass out.

But something worse happened. The top of her right hand swelled, numb and tingly, as though stung by a scorpion or rattlesnake. It grew as she watched.

"Excuse me…" she pleaded to the attendants, but they weren't paying attention. A middle-aged woman with perfect hair—why notice her hair?—saw Catherine's distress and tapped Sarmudio's elbow. He looked at her, then at Catherine, his eyes wide.

What did he see?

Self-conscious, Catherine touched her face, feeling the puffiness. Her cheeks were swollen.

"Miss Cho?" Sarmudio asked, approaching. "Are you okay?"

She tried to speak but realized her throat and tongue were also swollen. She shook her head, unable to form words.

The other attendant, Julia, hurried over. "I think she's having an allergic reaction," she said. Even up close, and knowing Julia was humani, Catherine couldn't tell.

"Indeed." Sarmudio checked the scanner. "Do you think it's from the gaiapentin?"

"Perhaps." Their voices were practiced.

"There have been no cases of anaphylaxis with gaiapentin," Julia said. "It must be…"

"The object."

"It must have been carrying … something."

The look they exchanged frightened Catherine.

"Everyone on board is going to need to be quarantined now. This is really bad."

"What is our next step in the procedure?" Sarmudio asked.

"I've never had a situation like this come up," Julia admitted.

Their attention returned to their scanners.

Catherine's body rebelled, pain erupting in every cell. Her thoughts turned against her, memories and emotions snowballing, burying her.

Voices filled her head, speaking in a language she didn't understand. Something had taken root in her consciousness. Her visitor, or visitors, communicated in ways she couldn't comprehend.

Looking down, she realized her fingers had fused into claws. Her pain felt distant, as though coming from another room.

Her vision widened, colors brightening as if under intense lighting. Her jaw felt bigger, her teeth pointed.

She was being remade. Into what, she didn't know. Her brain processed the situation lightning fast. *Fight it,* she thought. *You're infected by that asteroid. If you go to Sydney, you'll bring the infection with you. Is that what you want? To infect mom, too?*

But she was so hungry. Starving, like waiting hours for Thanksgiving dinner, the smell driving her crazy. *By the time you eventually eat, you overdo it and make yourself sick.*

The smell of the hot turkey from those faraway holidays sounded good, but she craved something more. Something still breathing. Meat still alive. *You'd do anything to feel full and satiated.*

Sarmudio and Julia backed away, along with the other passengers who cowered near the front of the craft.

"Don't be afraid. It's just me." Her voice was an impossibly deep guttural growl. The *Star Sailor* jolted, rolling port side, and she fell back toward her seat. Everyone screamed.

"Get back to your seats," Sarmudio hollered. "Buckle up."

"Not with that thing in here with us," a passenger said.

The ship rolled again, a loud humming filling the cabin. Outside the window, Catherine glimpsed a huge object rushing past. A meteor? An asteroid?

Thwack. Thwack. Thwack.

More screams. People clutching their stomachs, arms, and legs, bleeding from spots. More mini asteroids had breached the *Star Sailor*.

The ship banked left, giving a picture-perfect view of the asteroid heading toward Earth.

Movement on its surface, creatures that looked like evolved versions of what Catherine was turning into.

Cries filled the cabin as others began changing, too.

Maybe I've earned my fate ... maybe we all did.

The things had been observing and were putting them back in place.

"Thirteen kilometers," Sarmudio's voice was perfunctory. "The asteroid is thirteen kilometers. Larger than the one that killed the dinosaurs."

Would he and the other humani survive? Would any of them? "Twenty-two minutes until impact. How did we not detect this? It's as though it were launched at us… but by what?"

He looked up at Catherine, realization dawning. The thing that remade her was responsible. Her thoughts, now intertwined with theirs, understood. They had traveled too high, too far. They were being put in their place, reminded of the perimeters of their aviarium.

The other world Catherine glimpsed returned to her mind. Was it theirs? Did it belong to other civilizations they'd conquered? What did it mean for Earth?

It all felt inevitable.

Her stomach ached. She had to eat. The ramen had tipped over.

The others in the cabin were changed, too. And equally as hungry.

The humani were in pieces. A cruel trick.

Catherine took a final look out the window, gazing at the beautiful blue oceans below. The *Star Sailor* hit the atmosphere, and the windows turned yellow as the craft began reentry. Then red. Then white. Then blue. They were plummeting down, down, down.

A scene from *Wuthering Heights* came to her mind: a young Catherine being called a cunning little fox.

Why, yes. Yes, I am. And I'm about to rip apart your house and ruin your world forever.

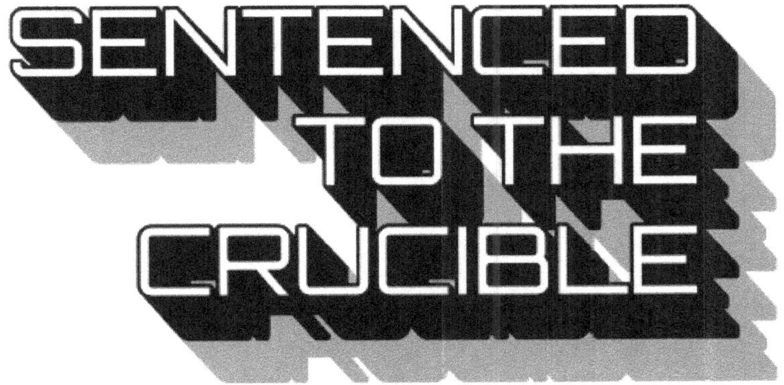

DAVID AGRANOFF

SPACE HORRORS

SENTENCED TO THE CRUCIBLE

DAVID AGRANOFF

THEY WOKE HIM A MONTH AFTER the slingshot out of the gravity well at Venus.

He expected to be on ice the whole way, but there was work to do. He wasn't there on vacation. The outer ring was hotter than the rest of the ship. The regular crew avoided that part, but it was where he was assigned. The internal gravity here was uneven, and during some shifts the fuel cell cases were heavier.

He asked his watch their location at the start of his shift. They were less than forty million miles from the sun. Mercury's orbit at the time was ten days from perihelion, the moment when it was closest to the sun. Most fuel-haulers wait until aphelion and Earth's orbit are on the same side of the sun but due to orbital quirks that wasn't happening for another EYear. The energy-hungry planets needed their fuel cells now. So, the pay was double for the crew of the *Oduduwa*, who were also making money shipping an unwilling workforce. He wasn't part of the crew.

The solar fuel cells generated on Mercury were the key to cooling Earth—and to the survival of the human race. Supply ships managed the journey no matter where Mercury was in its quick trip around the sun. Everyone had to make sacrifices.

Kevin Todd liked to tell himself he was ensuring his boys had a future, but they would never be able or willing to thank him for it. He was never given a choice. The crew of the ship, lifelong spacers, didn't even look at him. The directions and work orders came to his watch. The only time they spoke to him was to bark orders when he did something wrong.

"Eh, just lock up the cases and get your ass in drive!" one of the women who loaded the dock yelled at him.

Did they know or care that he was an engineer? They had him pushing pallets into place. The exchange of empty fuel cells for loaded ones took almost three EDays, sixty-eight hours, giving the *Oduduwa* a four-hour launch window to leave Mercury. The captain made it clear; her crew would get a bonus for every hour they skipped before the launch window.

Kevin locked the last empty fuel cell into the docking port, took a breath, and looked at his work. He didn't care if it wasn't perfect. What could they do to him now? The AI dock manager signaled that his shift was complete, and the door to the dock rattled open. He was doing something right because the primary door opened. It was a more direct route back to his cabin.

"KT-29034, you may not return to your cabin. Be advised your goggles are required as the observation port is currently open."

Kevin slid his goggles on. The light poured into the hall, even some distance from the window it was bright. The UV goggles protected him, but he was still blind in the bright glow. The ship sounded chimes for him to follow until he reached the rail that would guide him. The wall was hot, not as much as an oven coil, but warm. As he walked closer to the observation port, the goggles adjusted so that he could see two women standing by the observation port. They stared through goggles out into space.

As he got close, he could tell they were spacers, members of the crew. They were shorter, moving differently, more fluid, as if they had never lived in full gravity. But it was their eyes that had never adjusted to distance or natural light that creeped him out. He liked that they would always be behind goggles. He hated making eye contact.

As soon as he could see out the window. His mouth gaped involuntarily. It was like staring into a solar eclipse. The shape of the approaching planet blocked the star at forty million miles away, and the flaming corona came up behind the planet. It was a terrifying sight. The power of nature, the intensity felt soul-crushing, and the danger of it all gave him an ache in his stomach.

"Shit." One of the women at the window turned to leave. Kevin sensed her eyes on him as she departed. The woman who remained kept her eyes on the sight. It took him a minute to realize who she was. He had only seen her picture on the manifest, but it was Captain Abdebayo herself. He wanted desperately to say something. He was as nervous as he much as he was in awe of the sight.

"It is amazing," Kevin said. She didn't reply. "You know it has almost the same landmass as Amer…"

"No," Abdebayo shook her head. "Don't bother." She kept her eyes on the view.

"I'm sorry."

"Your guidelines were sent to your watch before launch."

Abdebayo turned and left. In her wake, anger floated in the air. It was a common reaction, and he'd felt it a hundred times. He stared at the planet surrounded by flames. It would blind him instantly if he removed the goggles. It was nothing compared to the feeling Abdebayo gave him. He was lucky looks didn't kill.

Kevin listened to her boots clunk away. That was the only human interaction he'd had since he came to the ship. Minutes passed, and he was mesmerized by the dance of the corona. He heard footsteps behind him, heavier and somehow different. The instinct was to be polite, to say hello. He understood the warning from the Captain. He was not supposed to talk to the crew.

He had bigger issues. In a few EDays, this ship would be loaded with solar-fuel cells charged on the sun-side of Mercury and launched back toward the central solar system, leaving him behind. He felt eyes on him. He could stand there mute if he had to. The other person was a few feet away.

"It's okay. I am not legally part of the crew."

Another transfer and he turned to smile at the person. He gasped and instantly felt guilty about it. It wasn't intentional; it just happened. They wore no goggles, basking in the light. It took him a few seconds to process this. It was a woman, and he thought she was blind. She looked like a normal woman, like the rest of the crew, but she was engineered. An android. The mechanical eyes were built with UV protection no human had. It had been a century since artificials were common in the central colonies and very out of style on Earth.

"I see that," Kevin whispered.

The artificials looked human, sounded human, could sometimes pass, but bad programming, in the hands of bad people, had made them a servant class that did dirty jobs, and worse. He was surprised to see one up close. He would never have guessed. Asimov's laws were nothing to self-learning AI, or programmers with bad intentions. Earth, Luna, and the Jovian colonies all had laws against artificials. Kevin wondered if this android was even on the manifest.

"You work on this ship?"

The android tipped her head slightly. "Since before the captain was born."

Kevin shook his head. The time spent working on this ship meant nothing. Out here the cruel indifference of the universe was a constant reminder. Free of the Earth, the frail threads of technology kept you alive. It was easy to discount the gift of life, and now he had the mission to try to survive on this hellhole.

"Thank you." Kevin smiled at the being before returning to his cabin for the landing.

***

The crew of the *Oduduwa* strapped in for the final approach. The announcement to prepare for landing filled him with dread. He knew they could pull it off; the crew had landed on Mercury many times before.

Kevin should've been in his bunk, but he looked out the window. The atmosphere was invisible, but they all felt it as they passed through. It shook the ship and rattled his teeth. The last hour as the surface grew closer, the craters became clear. He'd read about the danger ahead. They were landing in a crater the size of Ohio. It was a huge chunk of the entire world. The equator of the planet was only 3,032 miles around. He watched out a window as long as he could. He slid the goggles up. As they approached the landing site on the nightside of the planet, there was a glowing dawn on the horizon. It would fry his eyes if he stared at it. Crossing the center of Mercury, it looked like a road or path. Visible from sixty miles above the surface was the only building on the planet. It was his new home, or, more accurately, tomb.

It was a haunted world. Turning so slowly that one hundred and seventy-six days passed on Earth for one on Mercury. The dayside burned a hellish 800 degrees Fahrenheit, while the darkside froze at 270 degrees below zero. Shadowed craters held water in blocks of ice older than human civilization. Soon, he would drink the water harvested from the ancient ice. He would be left to live on a world so hostile to human life it was thought impossible to colonize.

Necessity is the mother of invention. The energy-hungry human population needed the solar energy constantly hitting the surface of Mercury. As he was told at his sentencing: *"No one lives on Mercury, but 262 men are dying there. And you Mister Todd will be one of them."*

The surface was coming up quickly. He went to his bunk and strapped in as the ship rattled violently around him. He closed his fists and prayed. Jammed between two cushions so he could see it when he lay down was the picture he smuggled in his sock. His sister gave him the picture on her last visit. Rachel in her red dress, which she liked to wear when they traveled. The boys, at the time, were seven and ten years old, each clutching a leg. It was their first family trip to orbit. The boys wanted to go to a ZeroG Park. It was the last time they were a happy family. When he wanted to die, he thought of this day. The happiness he had felt. This picture was his hope.

The ship shook until the last moment. A chime announced that they were on the ground. Kevin unstrapped himself. The gravity was only thirty-eight percent of Earth's, but after weeks in space, it felt like a weight holding him down. He was here. The journey was over, and he understood what was happening. Centuries ago, it would have been a gas chamber or a firing squad. North America was under religious rule, and execution was out of favor. This planet was supposed to claim his soul.

***

The airlock opened with a hiss like a giant letting out a deeply held breath. The hot stale air carried with it the smell of hundreds of men living under one roof. Kevin braced himself and wished he could stay in the tightly controlled environment of the transport. The loading dock would have fit two football fields. A large crew waited to start the transfer: the fuel cells had a slight glow to them. One lane spit out the empty cells, and another loaded the captured power of the sun.

The seal formed and a bell chimed. The workers started to move out pallets. Kevin pushed his pallet off the ship, the small amount of gravity fighting him. It was just enough that he felt a pain in his back as he put his head down and heaved.

"Oh hell no, don't help those bitches!" A skinny pale guy came up and yanked his arm. "You're a transfer, right?"

Kevin nodded. The man pulled him away from the pallet leaving it in the middle of the path. He had been white-skinned when he was born but now looked almost red, like a cartoon devil, minus the horns. The inflamed skin was painful to look at. His sun protection goggles were holding his graying hair back. He had a wicked tan line where the strap of the goggles blocked the sunlight.

"You don't work for them anymore." He looked at the women from the crew and pulled a finger across his neck. He talked as they moved away. "Welcome to the Crucible, also known as Icarus Detention Center. I know, everything has that name this close to the sun. Just so you know, prisoners call it the Ick. Politicians in the central system call it CCRC, The Children of the Crucible Rehabilitation Center, or work camp, depending on which funding bill you're reading, but I call it the steaming hot asshole of the solar system."

The man waited for Kevin to laugh; none of this was funny.

"Okay, no sense of humor. Well, I would love to tell you that you get used to the smell, but I can't."

Kevin didn't know what to say. No one had talked to him since Earth, not really since his trial—at least not like this. It was then that he realized he didn't feel the picture in his sock, wrapped in a plastic sandwich bag to keep sweat from destroying it. He'd left it in his cabin.

"Fine then. Alright new guy, let's start over. I'm Greg, a know-it-all motormouth, and that makes me your new best friend. I can show you the ropes, which is life or death when you're living on a barely habitable planet." Greg waited through an uncomfortable pause. "…and you are?"

Kevin heard some of the words he said, but he was thinking about running back into the ship. Then he realized this man Greg had asked him his name. "Uh, Kevin—"

"Wait, stop right there. No last names, you don't want to do that. No, no. Number one rule at the Ick, there are no last names. And never tell anyone why you're here. No *What are you in for* bullshit. It doesn't do anyone any good to know."

Greg let go of his arm and offered him a hand. Finally, they shook.

"I left a few things in my cabin." Kevin pointed back at the ship. A woman from the crew stood at the airlock with a rifle and a belt of bullets across her chest.

"Yeah, not happening, Kev. You could ask the COs." Greg let out a nervous laugh. "But the correction officers are just prisoners on 'good time.' Or you could ask the support staff, but they're hundred-year-old androids. Those fucking jalopies are kinda creepy. This means the transport crew doesn't really answer their questions either. And yes, at the Ick the Andys have rights and authority here. Whatever you did, and again I don't want to know, makes you lower than them…legally speaking. Your shit is gone, and no one cares."

Kevin kept staring at the airlock. He couldn't let go of it.

"What are we talking about a few shirts, underwear? You gotta get Ick issued. We'll grab you a bag on your way to your bunk. We just had one open up a week ago in our unit." Greg made a cross on his chest and looked up. "No cells here, dorm style, until you rack up good time, you make a year clean, maybe you'll get a cell."

"I just need a minute to go back." Kevin walked toward the ship.

"Come on man, what is so fucking important?"

"Pictures of my family, a couple of books."

"Family? That shit is a heartbreak man. I don't think you should've had those on you. Those pictures are contraband for legit reasons. And books, we got a library, but you'll be too tired to read."

The guard at the door of the ship was a serious woman. Kevin stopped short of her, and she shook her head.

"Fuck." Kevin took a deep breath.

Greg pulled on his arm. "Sorry, ma'am, my friend just wanted to thank you for the safe landing."

She clicked a warning. No words needed. Inside, Kevin's heart was breaking. He wondered if she would shoot him if he just ran past her. Greg stepped between them.

"Let it go, man." Greg pointed with his thumb. "Check in; they're gone."

Greg waved him to a hallway leading out of the docking port. An android guarded the hall. His artificial skin was peeling, and he looked a century old, barely functioning. His artificial hair survived only in patches. Decades ago, this being was built to fool people into thinking it was a human male, but harsh conditions and disrepair left it looking like a monster. Kevin could see several androids walking around them. One female android looked as if she was trying to maintain appearances, but several had rotted almost down to their exoskeletons.

"Hey, Officer, this is Kevin; he's an FNG." Greg turned and looked at Kevin. "No offense."

The android stepped in front of Kevin and looked at him. They made eye contact, and his robotic eyes glowed for a moment. "Identity confirmed." A prisoner came out holding a mesh bag with clothes. Kevin stared at the bag: a couple opairs of pants, shirts, a fresh pair of sun-blocking goggles.

"That's your laundry bag. Every five days—oh yeah, we do EDays 24 hours with 10-hour work shifts, 30 minutes for lunch, or the soup that passes for lunch—anyways, every five days, there are five units, each unit turns in their clothes, and they wash them in a huge vat," Greg explained.

"All together?"

"Yeah, that's nothing. You don't want to know about the water recycling around here. You an Earther?"

Kevin slung the clothes bag over his shoulder. The android pointed to his unit.

"Tell ops control I need five, uh cover me for ten, to show the FNG his new home." Greg clapped and pointed at the android.

They walked through a clear tube that went around the outside of the massive structure. The view was spectacular. The permanent dawn glowed with the light of the sun whose rise they stayed ahead of. Kevin stopped and took in the sight of the crater. The peaks were almost too far to see. He wondered about the view from deeper into the nightside. Greg tapped his foot a bit but let him stare. He must have understood the awe and wonder Kevin was feeling.

"Two miles an hour, if you stare long enough you can tell we're moving. We have to. The only livable spot in here is right here, in the day-night terminator. Since the planet moves slow, this whole fucking prison, a city block, is on wheels, massive wheels. They dug out a path through the craters, insane really."

Kevin knew why. It was big money harvesting energy from this world. It was also deadly. So who else could work this planet but people like him?

***

The sky never changed. Living on the slow-moving horizon had a rhythm, and Greg always reminded him it could be slower. Only Venus was slower, but no one lived on that hellhole. Kevin rolled out of bed as he did every artificially agreed-upon morning. He looked at the calendar on the wall that was smuggled in from a transport ship. He had traded a pair of socks for the ability to mark off each of the fifty-two days he'd already spent here. According to the Ick's Master control center, the EDay matched the time in the Bureau of Industrial Prisons headquarters in San Antonio, Texas. Give or take a time dilation or a transmission delay of eight minutes, they were synched with Earth. It was December 15, 2321.

He got out of pushing fuel cell pallets on his third day. The BOIP file finally uploaded, and management discovered he was a mechanical engineer in his past life. So now the workday was spent fixing androids. The activity in the unit was fifty men waking and all trying to follow their routine. Kevin would pour oatmeal into one of his two mugs; each day he walked to the hot waterspout and made instant oatmeal. Coffee went into the other. He passed Greg's bunk every morning on the way there, but Greg was up before 'lights on,' doing his bathroom routine before the rush. Fifty guys needed to pee with only fifteen toilets. It could easily look like roaches scattering with the lights, but they were all there long enough that they'd developed an unspoken system.

Greg normally was gone before Kevin passed his bunk. Today, he saw Greg still in bed, and Kevin got a bad feeling. The line at the hot waterspout was four deep; the same five guys met there every morning. Mikey P, who was quickly losing weight, and hair, shook his head as he passed Greg. He was a few days behind him. They silently waited for the hot water. There was nothing to say.

Once Kevin got enough hot water, he walked back to Greg's bunk and saw his coffee cup still half full from the morning before. Kevin sat in the chair at the tiny desk built into the unit across from Greg's bunk. Kevin stirred his oatmeal as Greg turned around. His eyes were sunken, his skin peeling. In ten days, he went from seeming okay to death's door.

"I don't want to know how bad I look."

"You look great."

"Please." Greg grinned. "These days all I can do is make turds, actual straight from the ass turds that feel good about themselves."

They both chuckled. The laughter sent a wave of pain through Greg's whole body. Kevin didn't have any way to reassure him. The new transport ships brought convicts almost as fast as Mercury chewed them up. The work was hard, as was the heat and radiation. It was impossible.

"I'd tell you to see a doctor." Kevin took a bite of his oatmeal.

"There's a reason they send the condemned here." Greg tried to sit up. "I pissed myself, but I can't get up."

"I'll help you."

"You gotta go fix Andys. You think you can cook up some skin? They're creeping everyone out," Greg said. Kevin couldn't tell him that the radiation was even harder on fake skin.

"You can't change yourself at this point, Greg."

"Dumbass, take a hint, let me die."

"Bullshit, Greg." Kevin wanted to argue that he should have some dignity here at the end.

"Kevin, I appreciate the kindness. I do." Greg smirked. "I don't deserve it."

Kevin took a swig of his coffee. He knew what Greg meant. They'd cared for each other for the last fifty-two days. They had talked, laughed, and from time to time felt human. It was a quick but intense friendship, like a booster that burned a fuel payload in seconds and died. They both understood this was an execution. Understanding that didn't make it easier. Kevin nodded. In his heart he didn't want to watch Greg die. He knew it was coming. They all wasted away here.

"Go fix your robots."

Kevin put his hand on Greg's bony shoulder. "Thank you, buddy, I mean..."

"Fuck off, I mean, you're welcome."

Kevin sipped his coffee. "I can stay if you want me to."

"Compassion is a bad look around here, Kev." Greg tried to smile but he no longer had the strength. "What did you do, Kev? To end up…"

His voice trailed off. Sometimes that was the hardest thing about living here. What the fuck did these people do to end up here? They seemed nice and normal, but Kevin knew full well what he did. He tried to tell himself that he was misunderstood. Maybe Greg felt the same; maybe he understood. He thought about it for a few heartbeats, but he couldn't bring himself to admit it to himself let alone Greg.

"The number rule of the Ick, Greg. I can't…"

He wasn't sure he wanted Greg to know, even now. Greg made a sound, not a death rattle, his body had no strength for that. His eyes locked on Kevin as his heart stopped. That was that.

***

The workshop was on the lowest level. He could feel the massive wheels churning that kept the Ick rolling. The sound of the fuel cells being lifted by magnets up into the building caused the walls to shake. It was easy to forget on the dorm levels that you were moving, but not down here. He knew Greg was dying the first time he met him, but he didn't expect to be there when it happened. The sound of the great motors felt extra crushing at this moment.

He opened the door to his workshop and wasn't surprised to find two androids. One he knew. A service droid who had been at the Ick for an EDecade. Synthetic flesh was rotting on its exoskeleton. This android had zero interest in talking; it didn't care about humans.

Kevin's heart skipped a beat when he saw the other. Fresh, a transfer. A transport ship had been here less than a week ago. She didn't know better. Most of the female-identifying androids understood it wasn't safe to look too much like a woman. It had only been fifty days, but it was still off-putting seeing a woman, artificial or not.

"Good morning." She looked like a teenager, with full red lips and blond hair in a cute pixie cut. *Was this a test?* Kevin was at a loss for words. She looked human. He would've thought she was human, but only Andys came into this office.

BR-4582STZ, in contrast, didn't resemble a person. It allowed itself to be identified only with a number. Kevin had told it to return after he printed a part for a new wrist joint. It was ready, sitting on the printer. BR-4582STZ got its part and left.

Kevin felt a rush of emotions, mostly fear. He felt the artificial woman's eyes on his back as the door closed. They were alone. He felt butterflies he didn't want. Nervous energy he didn't want. He told himself she wasn't real over and over.

"Do I call you Doctor?"

Kevin turned slowly. "Not a doctor." He stayed at the far end of the workshop.

"I'm a transfer."

Kevin shook his head. "I thought…"

"That criminal Andys were deactivated? Often yes."

Kevin knew they didn't have any rights. She sure looked human; by law she was supposed to have identifiable traits. Mechanical eyes, exposed circuitry, or tattooed Ident codes, which was why she was here. Kevin pulled up a chair and stared at her. She looked human; she looked young. Not many Andy manufacturers built teenagers or children anymore. He heard Neo-Tokyo had artificials in the clubs to encourage dancing.

Since he'd been arrested, no one had touched him or allowed him to touch them.

"My name is Cath. To fit regulations I need to be…visible."

Kevin reached up and touched her face. Her skin wasn't perfect but close enough. She had green eyes; they were human, had to be. He closed his eyes, just for a moment, and savored the feeling of her skin.

"What are you doing?" Cath sounded angry.

Kevin had spent the last few years afraid. From where she came from Cath was a being with no rights but on this world— He snapped his hand back.

240

"Your eyes, I can print you eyes." Kevin pointed at the goggles on her belt. "Won't need those anymore."

Cath nodded. Kevin smiled. He used his watch to forward her some options. She was scrolling through while Kevin watched her.

"I would prefer if you didn't stare at me like that."

"Excuse me?" Kevin said.

"I have full access to all prisoner records."

Kevin felt punched in the gut. "Let's just focus on the work at hand."

"Children of the Crucible claim only light this strong, this powerful, can cleanse your souls."

Kevin grinned. "They have no intention of cleansing; this is an execution."

Cath nodded. "Well, can you blame them?"

Kevin shook his head. "Why are you here?"

"Good question. I am in Earth terms one hundred and fifty years old, designed for clubs over-looking old Hong Kong, but I was designed with a learning engine."

"Illegal," Kevin pointed out to her.

"Exactly, and it is also illegal to flip my off-switch. Not too dissimilar to your situation. They can't execute you, not under the current religious order in America, but they can try to cleanse you in a place that will kill you."

Kevin understood. "Illegal to flip my off-switch."

Cath nodded. "Too bad."

He leaned back, a little nervous, and looked at the android. He wasn't expecting anger from a machine, but this one lived as a woman. This one was designed to learn from the experience.

The android leaned closer. "How do you live with yourself?"

Rachel asked him the same question when she presented the divorce papers. She also told him the boys chose not to visit him. His own father refused to come to court. The parents of his victims came to court. Ashley's mother screamed, *"She was just a child."* It still echoed in his mind. He didn't need this, not today, not after watching Greg's pain.

Kevin didn't want to feel her looking at him. He lowered his goggles; she would only see her own reflection. "Who says I can live with myself?"

He stood up but she grabbed his arm. "It's supposed to hurt."

Kevin fled into the engine room. He knew she was right. There was nowhere in the universe where his life mattered. It was supposed to hurt.

He dropped his goggles onto the deck and walked toward the horizon. This was the world where he belonged.

AUTHOR
BIOS

SPACE HORRORS

AUTHOR BIOS

MIKE D. MCCARTY has worked at some of the top makeup effects companies in the film industry, where he has served as both an artist and a show supervisor. He currently runs and manages Autonomous FX for his longtime friend Jason Collins. Their recent accolades include *The Bondsman, The Pitt, Westworld, Dead Ringers, Bladerunner 2049,* and *Pam and Tommy* which won an Emmy and a Makeup Guild Award. Mike has well over 200 film credits to his name since 1994. His first published short story "The Grieving Process" was bought by the streaming series *Creepshow for Season 4;* they also hired him to write the screenplay. The episode aired on Shudder and AMC+. He published his first novel *Werewolf Bloodlines: Gemini Rising* through Bad Moon Books in 2014.

Find him at **https://mikedmccarty.com.**

"I've always loved horror and I've never thought that galactic terrors have ever really gotten their proper time in the public eye. Sure, the *Alien* series was a hit and is still producing decent material these days. It was a heavy influence on me growing up, even the book by Alan Dean Foster, but there was never enough of it. I've always found that Good sci-fi horror is annoyingly rare. It seems like it's more common in video games than movies, with a few notable exceptions, such as *Event Horizon* or *Pandorum*, and of course, John Carpenter's Earthbound Sci Fi horror Classic, *The Thing*, which was super influential on the young Mike McCarty who snuck into the theater in 1982. It helped drive me to who I am today and what I do for a living."

VANESSA FOGG dreams of selkies, dragons, and gritty cyberpunk futures from her home in western Michigan. She spent years as a research scientist in molecular cell biology and now works as a freelance medical writer. Her writing has appeared in *Lightspeed, Podcastle, The Deadlands, GigaNotoSaurus, Neil Clarke's The Best Science Fiction of the Year: Vol 4,* and the Bram Stoker Award-nominated anthology *Unquiet Spirits: Essays by Asian Women in Horror.* Her debut collection *The House of Illusionists* is forthcoming from Interstellar Flight Press. For a complete bibliography and more, visit her website at **vanessafogg.com**.

Vanessa's favorite space horror movie is the first *Alien* movie.

ERIC J. GUIGNARD is an author and anthologist of dark and speculative fiction, operating from the shadowy outskirts of Los Angeles, where he also runs the small press **Dark Moon Books**. He's twice won the Bram Stoker Award, won the Shirley Jackson Award, and been a finalist for both the World Fantasy Award and International Thriller Writers Award. His latest fiction collection is *A Graveside Gallery: Tales of Ghosts and Dark Matters* (Cemetery Dance). Visit **www.ericjguignard.com** for more info.

Although Eric's story isn't necessarily space "horror," he does love space horror movies. *Event Horizon*, the *Aliens* franchise, and *Jason X* (seriously!) are all top picks.

KC GRIFANT is an award-winning Southern Californian author who writes speculative stories in the horror, fantasy, sci-fi and weird west genres. She authored the award-winning supernatural western *Monster Gunslinger* series and *Shrouded Horror: Tales of the Uncanny.*

She is editor of *Women of the Weird West,* and co-editor of *Dread Coast: SoCal Horror Tales and Of Terrors and Tombstones.* She has publications in dozens of podcasts, magazines and Stoker-nominated anthologies. She teaches genre and short story workshops and has been a moderator, panelist, or speaker at dozens of conferences and events. She is co-founder and co-chair of the Horror Writers Association San Diego Chapter and a Science Fiction & Fantasy Writers Association mentor. Aside from constructing imaginary worlds, she works as an award-winning science communicator and tries to keep up with two small wildlings.

Learn more at **www.KCGrifant.com**.

Favorite space horror: "This might be an obvious one, but I'm obsessed with the *Aliens* trilogy. I love how two intelligent, capable females are pitted against each other to survive."

DAVID AGRANOFF is a novelist, screenwriter, and Horror and Science Fiction critic. He is the Splatterpunk and Wonderland book award-nominated author of 12 books including the WW II Vampire novel *The Last Night to Kill Nazis*, the science fiction novel *Goddamn Killing Machines* from CLASH BOOKS, the Cli-fi novel *Ring of Fire*, *Punk Rock Ghost Story*, and *People's Park* from Quoir books. As a critic he has written more than a thousand book reviews on his blog Postcards from a Dying World which has recently become a podcast, featuring interviews with award-winning and bestselling authors such Stephen Graham Jones, Paul Tremblay, Alma Katsu and Josh Malerman. For the last five years David has co-hosted the Dickheads podcast, a deep-dive into the work of Philip K. Dick, reviewing his novels in publication order, as well as the history of Science Fiction. His non-fiction essays have appeared on Tor.com, NeoText, and Cemetery Dance. His most recent novel is the science fiction novel *Great America in Dead World* which you can buy now! He just finished writing a book, *Unfinished PKD*, on the unpublished fragments and outlines of Philip K. Dick.

You can find Dickheads at **https://www.youtube.com/@DickHeadsPodcast.**

David's Book reviews and information can be found at **davidagranoff.blogspot.com.**

David Agranoff's favorite space horror novel Is Philip K. Dick's *The Three Stigmata of Palmer*

Eldritch; his space horror movie that isn't *Alien* is *Pitch Black*.

JON COHN is a horror novelist and professional board game designer. His works include the 2024 Indie Book Brawl Quarter-Finalist *Slashtag*, and the much less popular, but award-winning novel *The Island Mother*. He gets his best ideas from a tarot reader who lives in Hawaii.

As a designer, Jon is very excited to finally be able to merge horror books and games together by bringing *Ghostland* to life as a board game. He's also designed games like *Thanksgiving*, co-designed with Eli Roth, *Basket Case*, and *Taboo Horror*. Order autographed books and get updates for new games and upcoming novels at **www.joncohnauthor.com**. Sign up for the newsletter for free short stories and games, and follow at @joncohnauthor on Facebook, Instagram and TikTok.

Jon lives in San Diego with his supernaturally patient wife Delaney, and their adorable dog, Miss Cordelia Chase.

Favorite space horror book: "*Dead Silence* by S.A. Barnes is, for my money, the perfect space horror novel. Adrift on a haunted spaceship, this mashup of *The Shining* and *Aliens* is a master class in existential claustrophobia."

JOHN PALISANO's writing has won the Bram Stoker Award®, the Yog Soggoth Award, been nominated for the Rondo Hatton Award, and the Imajinn Award and has been published and appeared in such notable venues as *Vanity Fair, The Los Angeles Times*, Blumhouse Online, *Cemetery Dance, Fangoria*, and more. His screenplays have won acclaim as finalists in Shriekfest, Project Greenlight, Latent Image, and more. His professional career started with an internship and work with Ridley Scott & Associates, then with director Marcus Nispel, Tony Bon Jovi, and more. He recently served as President of the Horror Writers Association.

Find him at **www.johnpalisano.com**.

"My favorite space horror world is *Alien*. The original had a profound influence on me when I first saw at as a much too young child at our local drive in theater in Norwalk, Connecticut. It scared me and intrigued me and was the catalyst that set me on my journey. I still love the *Alien* world today."

KATHRYN BLANCHE In addition to writing, Kathryn can also be found traveling around the world, working in the theatre, and indulging her love of martial arts and stage combat. Kathryn finds that training in historical fencing as well as stage combat improves her ability to describe fights in her books and clears her mind. She has trained with professionals from Los Angeles to New York, and even as far away as London and Moscow.

Kathryn often spends her time with family and friends, catching up on the latest Sci-Fi and Fantasy films, and supporting local theaters. She owes her love of reading to her father, who introduced her to the fantasy genre when she was six years old and has since then constantly had her nose stuck in a book ever since.

Kathryn loves many horror elements common to sci-fi stories set in space, particularly ghost ships. But the most impactful space horror for her is the movie *Annihilation* due to the way the film blends the known with the unknown in both a beautiful and terrifying way. Also, because it raises the question of how different other life in the universe may be compared to what we are familiar with.

The first book in her dystopian fantasy series is *Caught by Demons: Laila of Midgard Book 1*, which is now available in print, ebook, and audiobook formats. It follows special agents in post-apocalyptic Los Angeles fighting supernatural crime. For more information, check out **www.kathrynblanche.com** or follow her on social media.

Facebook: @LailaofMidgardSeries
Instagram: @kathryn_blanche

VINCENT V. CAVA is an author who specializes in the field of horror. His work has been published by Simon & Schuster, PS Publishing, Shortwave Publishing, and more. He is the co-writer, co-producer of the *Creepypasta* film (2023). He's written two graphic novels, and his work has been used to promote film and television for Fox, Starz, and Crypt TV. His works are available where books are sold.

Find him at **www.vincentvenacava.com**.

"'The Second Variety' by Philip K Dick is not only the most terrifying sci-fi story I've ever read, but for my money, the single scariest piece of fiction ever written. A tale that still resonates with audiences today, it reminds us of the horrors of AI and drone warfare and paints a harrowing vision of what the future may look like if we don't put safeguards in place to protect ourselves. I come back to this piece every now and then and it never disappoints. Everyone knows PKD was truly a master of the science fiction genre, but his horror has always been underrated. Few in literature have been able to blend the two as effectively and diabolically as he could."

E.S. MAGILL fell in love with horror when she was very young, right after watching *Night of the Living Dead* when she was seven. Today, she writes dark fantasy and horror. Her novel *Magica: Book 1 Rise of the Cult* was a semi-finalist for the Mary Shelley Award for Paranormal Fiction. Her short stories have been published in anthologies, such as *California Screamin'* and *Blood Lite III*. In addition to writing, she has edited four anthologies of horror stories. She is also a mental health advocate, writing about her own journey in the nonfiction self-help book *Reveal Your Wings*. She holds a B.A. and M.A. in English and is a retired English teacher. Visit **www.esmagill.com** for more info and to join her reader community.

"When it comes to space horror, my favorite is *Event Horizon*. It's a combination of hard science and hard horror. The horror isn't monster or alien based but psychological. The film demonstrates how the effects of space and science can impact the human mind. Ultimately, the film reveals the horrible mysteriousness of the universe and the hubris of humans who think they can master it."

Thank you to all the writers who contributed to this anthology. You were all so great to work with.

I also want to thank my cover designer who always comes through with a cover that exceeds my vision.

And I'd like to thank you, the Reader, because it is through you a book comes alive.

If you enjoyed this book, please leave a review at
Amazon, BookBub, GoodReads,
or your favorite review site.

Turn the page to learn more about the writers.

SPACE HORRORS

VANESSA FOGG

SPACE HORRORS

KC GRIFANT

SPACE HORRORS

VINCENT V. CAVA

SPACE HORRORS

KATHRYN BLANCHE

SPACE HORRORS

JOHN PALISANO

SPACE HORRORS

JON COHN

SPACE HORRORS

MIKE D. McCARTY

SPACE HORRORS

ERIC J. GUIGNARD

SPACE HORRORS

E.S. MAGILL

David
Agranoff
novelist, podcaster,
screenwriter, critic

DAVID AGRANOFF
PEOPLE'S
PARK

GREAT AMERICAN DEAD WORLD
DAVID AGRANOFF

"David Agranoff is a razor sharp
writer, a storyteller with hard rock
pacing, a magician of ideas...An
idealist in hell."

-John Shirley, cyberpunk legend
and screenwriter of The Crow

Find him at:

https://www.facebook.com/DAgranoffauthor
https://davidagranoff.blogspot.com
https://www.youtube.com/@Veganrevwithzombies
https://www.youtube.com/c/dickheadspodcast

Horror, Bizarro, and Sci-Fi

David Agranoff
THE LAST
NIGHT
TO KILL

SPACE HORRORS

9 781961 502123